Pay Day

By ReShonda Tate Billingsley

and

Richelle Denise

BROWN GIRLS BOOKS

Houston, Texas * Washington, D.C.

Pay Day © 2015 By ReShonda Tate Billingsley and Richelle Denise

Brown Girls Books,

LLC   www.BrownGirlsBooks.com

ISBN: 9781625178312 (Digital)

9781625178329 (Print)

First Brown Girls Books LLC trade printing

Manufactured and Printed in the United States of America

4

Letter from Richelle

I am so grateful that God has allowed me to begin my journey as a writer. I have been put in the pathway of some very generous ladies who have been more instrumental to me than they know. Thank you to my mentor, Victoria Christopher Murray and her partner, ReShonda Tate Billingsley for believing in my writing abilities enough to help me begin my journey as a writer.

Thanks to my family and friends for every prayer and ounce of support you all have given me to pursue my writing career. Jayden and Landen, thanks for the inspiration the two of you give me...even though you guys don't realize it.

And, thanks to all of the readers for purchasing and being supportive.

Until the next book - thank you, thank you, thank you.

Richelle

Letter from ReShonda

As an author, I love telling great stories. And I've been so blessed to be able to make a living doing what I love. Life as an author is rewarding, fulfilling, and yes, sometimes, even frustrating. But I wouldn't trade it for anything. And this journey is made that much sweeter when there is someone along to enjoy the ride.

Unfortunately, with changing times, many aspiring authors are finding it hard to break into the industry. That's why it gives me great pleasure as publisher of Brown Girls Books to nurture and develop new talent.

When I started Brown Girls Publishing along with Victoria Christopher Murray, our goal was to give fan favorites and fresh voices a chance to bring their stories to the masses. We discovered so many talented writers, but there were a few who stood out from the crowd, who we truly wanted to take under our literary wings and watch them soar.

I am happy to present to you one of those writers.

Richelle Denise is a fresh voice that Brown Girls is presenting as part of our mentoring partnership. I was amazed at her talent, her tenacity, and her commitment to bring the best story possible to you. I know she is destined for great things. I hope you enjoy OUR story!

ReShonda

Chapter 1

Janine

How in the world was I supposed to focus on work? How in the world did a person go back to greeting irate customers when her world had been ripped to shreds?

But I had to do it. If I wanted to keep a roof over my head and feed my ten-year-old son, William, I had to wrap up my pity party, put on my big girl panties, and get over the fact that my husband of nine years had left me for his twenty-one-year-old kickboxing instructor.

I inhaled. Exhaled, then cursed when it didn't relax me like I'd hoped.

"Just let it go," I mumbled before brushing my spiral curls out of my face, slipping on my headset, and pressing the button to take my first call of the day. "Thank you for calling Clearcast, this is Janine Weathers. How may I assist you?"

"You can tell me why the hell my TV ain't working!" the female voice bellowed.

I closed my eyes, inhaled again, opened my eyes, and forced a pleasant response. "Our system has already identified you, but if you would please give me the last four digits of your social security number, I can be of further assistance."

"4-3-1-1," she belted out.

"I'm sorry, that's not what we have on file."

"Oh, I mean 3-9-8-6," she quickly corrected.

I couldn't help but roll my eyes. I'd bet five dollars 3-9-8-6 was her kid's social security number. Little Junie probably had no idea that he had premium cable in his name.

I tapped the keyboard and waited for the caller's account details to pop up on the screen. "Ma'am, your services were disconnected for non-payment," I told her.

She gasped like she was shocked. "Unh-unh, y'all didn't get my check?"

No, because you know your trifling tail didn't send it. "No ma'am. We have not received payment. You had a promise to pay on the 15th, but it wasn't paid."

"Unh-unh, I sent in my payment! I can't help it that y'all didn't get it," she snapped.

I imagined some ghetto chick sitting at home in her pink sponge rollers, a Newport cigarette dangling from her mouth, still in her housecoat even though it was almost eleven. "You need to take that up with the postal service," she continued. "All I know is you betta cut my

—

8

cable back on before 'The Young & the Restless' comes on because Victor is supposed to find out the baby ain't his. . ."

The woman rambled on as I leaned back in my chair. I swear, not a day passed that I didn't get some nutcase caller like this. They made me absolutely hate my job. "Ma'am, as soon as you pay your balance of 432 dollars, we will be more than happy to restore your services."

"I don't have 432 dollars!"

"But you sent us a check, right? So why don't you put a stop payment on that check and pay us with those funds?" I'm sure she could hear the smirk in my voice.

"Why don't you kiss my crack?" she screamed, as she proceeded to hurl obscenities at me.

I don't know if it was that last curse word, the fact that she was screaming at me, or if I had just reached my limit - four days of crying would do that to you - but I snapped.

"Look, if your ghetto fabulous behind had paid your cable bill instead of getting your blonde crochet braids done, your service wouldn't get cut off! Just put the cable in your other illegitimate kid's name and open a new account! But the bottom line is, if you can't pay your freakin' bill maybe you don't need cable!"

"Trick, you done lost your mind!" she screamed. "I ain't even got no braids."

"You *ain't got no* cable either, until you pay your bill," I said, mocking her poor grammar.

"Awww, hell naw!" She was full-metal jacket crazy now. "You must not know 'bout me! I will come up there and. . . Matter of fact, what is your name again? I'm on my way now!"

"My name is Puttin' Tang. Ask me again and I'll tell you the same." I pressed the End button and hung up the phone. Yes, she'd call back and ask to speak to a manager, but at this point, I didn't care. I put my phone on "Away" and headed to the break room. I'd never in my six years at this company been so rude, but a person can only take so much. And I was about six blocks past all that I could stand.

"Hey, girl," I said to my friend, Angelique, as I walked into the large room where Clearcast employees escaped the madness. She was squeezed into one of the chairs at a table in the corner. "What's going on?" I asked, taking in all the people laughing and mingling. It was only eleven a.m., so I was a little shocked at the number of people scattered around the room. There was cake and balloons like it was some type of celebration.

"Girl, Terrance and Sheray got married in Vegas this past Saturday. She finally got him to tie the knot. They just got back today after staying an extra three days for their honeymoon." Angelique shook her head. "She's better than me, though. Ain't no way I'd be with a guy for seven years before he decides to marry me."

"That's because your man would marry you yesterday if you'd just say the word." I laughed. Angelique dated a wonderful guy named Marcus, who loved every ounce of her full figure. But she always made excuses about needing to lose weight before she could even think about getting married.

At that moment, Terrance came strolling over. Even though both he and Sheray worked at Clearcast, we were primarily friends with him. We'd all been in the same training class when we started and had remained good friends since then. With chiseled abs and smooth dark skin, Terrance was by far one of the best looking guys working here, which is probably why Sheray transferred here from the downtown office last year.

"What's up?" Terrance said.

I looked at him, then down at his glass, which was filled with a liquid that looked a little too dark to be fruit punch. I leaned in and sniffed his glass. I coughed. "Dang, you spiking the punch this early?"

He nodded, took a sip, then said, "Yep. It's five o'clock somewhere. Plus, I'm still trying to get used to the fact that I'm married." He held his cup in the air. "And this helps me cope with my loss."

Angelique and I both squinted with confusion. I was the one to speak. "I don't get it. What did you lose?"

Terrance shook his head. "My freedom. I lost my right to date other women. You women just don't understand that marriage is like getting a life sentence. The same woman for the rest of your life." He took another long drink. "Sorry, that doesn't excite me."

"But didn't you propose to her?" Angelique asked.

"Only because she kept harassing me. Shoot, I stayed drunk the whole time in Vegas."

"Okay then, why did you get married?" I asked. I could tell Terrance sensed my irritation and Angelique snickered at my snappy tone. With all that I had endured in my personal life, I had no tolerance for a man who did not take marriage vows seriously.

He looked at me sideways. "In an effort to step out of the hot seat, I'm going to go ahead and change the subject. How are you feeling?" he asked. "I heard you were sick the past few days."

That's the lie I'd told everyone. But really I was just emotionally distraught because of Tony's abandonment. Nine years together and last week, over dinner, he just blurted out that he no longer wanted our marriage to continue. He even admitted that he was seeing someone else, Vlanka, the perky kickboxing instructor. His words had stunned me to my core. I knew that things had been strained between us, but I'd never suspected an affair – let alone an affair that would cause him to want to leave his family.

"Janine, you and I both know this isn't working," he told me.

I'd stared at him like he had two heads. "I don't know anything, except my husband has been distant and acts like it disgusts him to touch me."

I'd first noticed the widening distance between Tony and I about six months ago. We both worked crazy hours, me at Clearcast and him at the post office. Any free time we had, was spent with our son. I thought the distance was just normal marriage stuff. I had no idea that it was to the extreme of him wanting out.

"So you're leaving us to be with her?" I asked.

"I'm leaving, but she's not the reason," he replied.

I had wanted to shove the plate of smothered chicken, mashed potatoes, and green beans that I'd spent all evening cooking in his face. But rather than being violent, I just took all his hip hop gear and tossed it out on the lawn.

"Hello, did you hear me?" Terrance's voice snapped me back to this week. "I said, how are you feeling?"

"I'm cool," I said, trying to push away thoughts of my marriage and its abrupt ending. "I guess I missed a lot while I was out," I told him.

"Yep," he solemnly said.

I looked at my friend. I really liked Terrance and we were probably the closest of our little group. There was nothing sexual between us, because I was married and he had a girlfriend. But we were both sports fanatics, loved to laugh and although I was older than him, we instantly connected. That's why I couldn't understand why he was standing here looking like a kid who'd just had his Build-A-Bear taken away.

Angelique squeezed Terrance's hand. "Newlyweds are supposed to smile."

He gave her a side-eye and took another swig of his drink, then he grimaced as if the punch from the liquor almost k-o'd him.

"Okay, Terrance, what's really going on? I know you. And you don't seem the least bit happy about this marriage," Angelique said.

He looked at her crazy. "Did you not just hear me? I'm not happy."

"Then, I repeat, why did you get married?" I asked. He stood there like I'd just asked him the final question on a game show. "Well?" I folded my arms and waited for his response.

He sighed. "It was her birthday, we were having fun, got drunk, and I woke up with a wife."

"What?"

"I got got." He glanced across the room at Sheray, who was laughing it up with some of our coworkers. "I mean, I do love Sheray and everything, but you know that she can be a bit overbearing sometimes."

"You know you can get that annulled?" I told him.

"I know," Terrance continued, "but she cried and boo hooed and said she was tired of waiting. She'd be devastated if I broke it off. So what the hell?" He shrugged and downed the last of his drink.

"But you are always talking about you aren't ready to settle down," I replied.

"What am I supposed to do?" he asked. "Look at her." He motioned across the room to Sheray. She glanced our way, waved, and blew Terrance a kiss.

He gave a half smile, nodded his head, and pretended to catch the kiss.

I waved at her, then turned to Terrance. "I assume this shindig was her idea?"

Terrance nodded. "Yeah, she's the one that showed up with cake and ice cream to celebrate. Who does that?"

"You're married now. There's nothing you can do if you're not going to get it annulled so you may as well suck it up," Angelique told him.

Angelique Logan had actually gotten both of us a job with the company. She had been friends with Terrance since high school and I knew her because we got our hair done at the same salon. When she heard Clearcast was hiring, she had put in a good word for us both.

"I guess you're right," Terrance said. "I just need to suck it up."

I turned to Angelique. "Are you going out for lunch?"

"Yeah, I gotta pick up the lotto tickets. The jackpot is $62 million."

Me, Angelique, Terrance and two other co-workers, Raquelle and Owen had been doing a lotto pool at work for the past year. I knew it was a pipe dream, but one day out of the week I gave up my Starbucks for lotto, so it's not like I was just blowing money.

"Owen isn't playing this week, he said he's getting tired of wasting money so he's out." Angelique held out her hand toward Terrance. "What about you? Are you still in?"

"Yeah." He reached in his pocket and pulled out a five and handed it to Angelique just as Sheray bounced up.

"Hey, guys," she sang as she linked arms with Terrance and snuggled up against him.

"Hey," Angelique and I said simultaneously.

The smile left her face when she noticed the five dollars Terrance had just handed Angelique. "Whatcha doing, Baby?"

"Giving Angelique money for the lotto pool. It's Wednesday. You know we play every week," he replied.

Sheray narrowed her eyes at Terrance. "Baby, we agreed that we were on a budget now." Then, she looked at me and Angelique and gave us what I assumed to be a forced smile. "We're saving for our future."

Terrance stared at her in disbelief. "It's five dollars," he said.

"Yes, but five dollars every week adds up." She smiled as she patted his cheek. "We have a future to think about now so that means no frivolous spending." She flashed another fake smile at us, then leaned in and kissed him on the cheek. "I'm going to get going. I'm supposed to meet the realtor in forty-five minutes. Aren't you going to walk me out?"

He looked like he wanted to go off on her, but he just said, "Give me a minute."

Sheray turned to us. "See you ladies later."

We gave her a half-hearted goodbye, then looked at Terrance after she left. Sheray had been like that since they began dating. She never wanted anyone to know when they weren't seated front and center on the happy train. She loved Terrance so much that she didn't care about anything but being with him.

"Wow," I said.

"Are you guys buying a place?" Angelique asked.

"No, she's selling her condo because she moved in my place." He let out a heavy sigh. "We didn't even talk about it. I think that's what's bothering me. It's like she just took over my life. And now she's even trying to regulate how I spend my money."

Angelique attempted to hand him the five back. "Maybe you need to sit out the pool."

17

"Whatever. I'm in. I work every day. If I want to spend five dollars, I'm spending five dollars." He shook his head in frustration as he headed toward the door.

"Well, I got everybody's money. Since Owen is out, I'll only get twenty tickets instead of twenty-five," Angelique said once Terrance was gone. I'd given her ten dollars last week, so I was covered. "Raquelle gave me her money right before they called her into the office, so I'll go ahead and make this run before Evelyn comes hunting me down," she said, referring to our supervisor.

As if we'd talked her up, Evelyn stuck her head in the break room.

"Janine, may I have a word with you?" Her tone let me know that ghetto-lady had indeed called back and they'd traced it back to me.

I sighed heavily. "Coming. . . "

"What are you in trouble for?" Angelique whispered as I was walking off.

"I cussed out a customer," I said with a raised brow.

"You'd better lie and say you didn't," she called after me.

I nodded. She was right. Cussing out customers was grounds for immediate termination. If I had any tears left, I probably would've cried because I needed my job – especially now that I was a single mother. Yep, I needed to play dumb because I definitely couldn't get fired now.

Chapter 2

Raquelle

*T*his could not be happening, I kept mumbling to myself as I struggled to keep from rocking back and forth. But judging from the look on Mr. Perry's face and the two other men perched behind him, there was no doubt, it was definitely happening.

The disdain on my boss's face made me feel like a child who had let down her parents.

"To say that I am disappointed is an understatement," Mr. Perry said. "You have been a trusted member of this team for eight years. A valued employee and you would dare do this?"

I pushed back the tears that were fighting to make their escape.

"We gave you extended time off to deal with your son." Mr. Perry's voice was stern and unwavering. "We worked with you when you ran out of sick days. I tolerated your tardiness, your excuses and this is how you repay me?"

"I know that no words can excuse what I did," I finally managed to say.

"You are absolutely right about that."

"But. . . I was desperate."

"You know," Mr. Perry said, "that's what I kept telling myself. That if this prized employee that I know and trust could do something like this, it could only mean that she was desperate. So I did some research of my own." He glanced down at a stack of papers in front of him. "I see insurance – that I pay a huge chunk of – covered most of your son's treatment. The rest totaled about 65-thousand dollars."

I had no idea how he had access to my financial information. But who was I kidding? He was Lawton Perry, one of the richest entrepreneurs in Houston and the founder of Clearcast Cable. He could buy any information he wanted.

"So, I'll give you the 65-thousand," Mr. Perry continued. He pounded the papers on his desk. "But please explain to me where the other 125-thousand came into play?"

I opened my mouth but no words came out. There were no words to justify what I'd done. I was a former honor roll student, turned thief. I'd been a supervisor in the accounting department for the past five years. Two years ago, after seeing how much money was coming into Clearcast and the lack of oversight, I'd started syphoning off cash, making out checks to myself. At first, they were small checks, but when no one noticed, they grew each time. Soon, the easier it got to take the money, the harder it was to stop. And sixty thousand became eighty. Eighty became 100. 100 became 125 and honestly, I probably would've kept going if a surprise audit hadn't derailed my spending.

I'm not really a thief. Well, I never was until desperation drove me there and dropped me off with an unmonitored pass to syphon off money. But now, it looked like I was about to pay the ultimate price.

"Mrs. Vargas, what do you think should happen?" That came from the HR director, Harry, who had been standing silently behind Mr. Perry the entire time.

I had barely sat down at my desk this morning when I'd been summoned into the boss's office. We usually had staff meetings on Wednesday afternoons, so I'd been praying that he wanted to talk to me in regard to something about the meeting. But my gut said otherwise. When you're doing dirt, any word from the higher-ups can send your nerves into a frenzy. That's why I'd had to duck in the bathroom and calm myself down before I made my way up to the twelfth floor and into Mr. Perry's massive office.

"They don't know, they don't know," I'd repeatedly mumbled to myself. But as soon as I walked into that office, I knew that they knew.

"Answer him," Mr. Perry said. "What do you think should happen now?"

I wanted to tell them that I wanted them to pretend this never happened. To let me go on about my merry way and I'd never steal another dime from anyone. But I knew that would never be an option.

"I, I can pay it back," I stammered.

"Okay." Mr. Perry casually held out his hand. "Give it here. All of it."

I swallowed the lump in my throat. I may have had a few thousand in the bank, well not a few. It was more like a couple. My nine-year-old son, Shaun, had been diagnosed with kidney failure. I took the first ten thousand to cover his mounting medical bills. Then there was the experimental treatment that didn't work. Sam, my children's father and my husband of six years, died three years ago, so I was doing all of this on my own. In the beginning, the money was just for Shaun. But once he got better, I wanted to do more. I wanted to celebrate life and I'd gotten caught up. I spent the money I'd taken more frivolously than I should have. My kids and I started living pretty well. We took vacations, and I bought Shaun all of the latest Jordan's, along with any jersey that came out. My teenage daughter, Tiana, and I had regular appointments for mani's, pedi's, and spa treatments because I thought it was important that she didn't get lost in all the attention that I gave to Shaun. I finally came to my senses and figured I should put the extra money to good use. I'd put a down payment on our house, I bought a new car, and just enjoyed life as an upper class woman. Shaun got better and the money got good. Then, Shaun took a turn for the worse, requiring a kidney transplant and that was my justification for bumping up the fake checks to five figures.

"I-I don't have the money right now."

"Of course you don't," Mr. Perry said, gathering his papers up.

"But I can get it. I can pay you back," I cried.

"How will you do that when you don't have a job?" he replied.

The tears I'd been holding back finally escaped. I don't know why I thought, why I hoped that they wouldn't fire me.

"Surely, you don't think I was going to keep you employed here." He stood up.

"Please, Mr. Perry, let me work it off."

"Mrs. Vargas, there are two things I absolutely abhor. A liar and a thief. If you had come to me and explained the situation about your son, I would've been more likely to help you. Now, I have no sympathy for you." He sneered at me as he finished with, "Please exit my building."

Security eased over to me. "Mrs. Vargas, your belongings have been packed up," Harry, the HR director said as the guard helped me stand. "Dante will escort you to your office to retrieve your immediate personal items, then he'll escort you out of the building. You should be grateful that Mr. Perry chose not to arrest you on the spot. I do, however, suggest that you get an attorney."

"An attorney?"

"Yes," Harry said. "We will be filing embezzlement charges. You're looking at some serious jail time."

I collapsed back in my chair. Embezzlement? Jail? What would happen to my children?

"No, please. I'm so sorry," I cried.

All of the men began gathering up their belongings, basically dismissing me. I could tell my tears moved none of them. And then, reality set in. Without this job, not only would I not have money, I wouldn't have any benefits. How was I supposed to pay for Shaun's kidney transplant? He was on a waiting list, but if he got a donor soon, we'd need to get it done as soon as possible.

I begged, "Please, Mr. Perry, don't press charges. I promise, I'll pay back every penny no matter how long it takes. I need this job. My son's life depends on it."

Dante, the security guard, whispered, "Come on, Raquelle, let me help you out." I could tell he was trying to be gentle and me acting a fool would only make things worse so I just bowed my head in shame as I stood and let him escort me out.

Tears streamed down my face as I let him lead me down the long hall, past the elevator and to my office. The place that I had worked for the past eight years became a blur as I walked toward my office. As I waited for the door to open, I prayed none of my friends were at their desks. In fact, I wished I had access to a phone so I could call in a bomb threat or something. Anything so that my friends and coworkers wouldn't see my shame as I was escorted out the building like a common criminal.

My mother always said, "Greed has been the death of many a man." And now, because of my greed, my son could very well die.

Chapter 3

Angelique

Terrance's party had wrapped up. I knew because I'd poked my head back in so I could snatch a piece of that delicious looking banana pudding cake. I had been overweight all my life, so I was very self-conscious about eating sweets in public. The cake was sitting on a back table, calling my name. I smiled as I approached what was left of the sheet cake.

I released a euphoric sigh as I scooped up a piece and popped it in my mouth. Just as I did that, I looked up to see Marcus, my live-in boyfriend of four years. Marcus was a field tech for Clearcast and was almost never in the office. So, why he would be here now, just as I was about to gnaw down on this cake? This had to be some kind of cruel joke.

Marcus was one of the good guys. He loved me like little girls dreamed of being loved. It wasn't that I didn't feel the same way, because I did. I loved him, but sometimes my insecurities caused me to push away from him.

Just a week ago, I agreed to us going on a strict diet to shed some of the pounds. Marcus didn't have a weight problem, yet he agreed to make healthy eating choices so that it would be easier for me to do the same. Everyone that knew us, knew that Marcus loved me and he would do anything in order to protect me. So not only did everyone love him, he was handsome and looked just like that actor Lahman Rucker, but they loved the way he treated me. That's why I felt like Tyler Perry stole my story in that "Why Did I Get Married" movie. I was Jill Scott, minus the singing, of course. I wasn't bad-looking at all, but I did have a good one hundred pounds over Marcus. It bothered me, but not him. I just never understood why someone of his caliber would fall for someone like me.

The look on his face was one of disappointment when he spotted me with the cake. His expression was enough to make me grab a napkin, spit the piece of cake back into the paper, and toss it in the trash.

"Angelique. . ."

I turned and darted out of the break room before he could finish his sentence. I ducked into the restroom, pushed into a stall, and let the tears flow. It was hard for me to understand why I didn't have will power. If Marcus hadn't walked in, I probably would've eaten everything that was left. And that made me ashamed. Why did someone else have to look at me in a certain way for me to put the cake down? Why couldn't I want better for myself on my own?

Finally, I walked out of the stall, wiped my eyes and looked in the mirror.

You're pretty for a big girl.

The words rang in my head. I used to believe that needed to be my national anthem. My mother – God bless her warped, dysfunctional soul – told me that on a daily basis. I think she was trying to make me feel good about myself. But it hadn't worked. I stared at myself in the mirror. All 285 pounds of my 5'6" frame.

The one thing my mother's "You're pretty for a big girl" comment had done, was given me low self esteem. Growing up, it got to the point where I learned to hide how much the fat jokes bothered me. I'd even learned to crack a few of my own. But my self-esteem had been taking a beating over the last few years because my self worth tanked with each pound. Yes, I had Marcus, but I had a hard time accepting his love. I knew it was because I felt inferior to other women.

People just didn't get it. I'd tried every diet ever invented. Although, I had a sweet tooth, I wasn't some ferocious eater. I'd like to think my metabolism was slower than most people's. And yes, I'd diagnosed myself and found that I was severely allergic to exercising. So, yeah, I knew part of my weight was my own fault, but as soon as I got enough money, I was going to have gastric bypass surgery. I'd already checked into it and this bootleg insurance at Clearcast wouldn't cover it, so I'd have to come up with $14,000 on my own. So far, I had about $3,000 saved.

I shook off my tears and took my big behind back outside. I knew Marcus would give me my space. He knew my struggle and was amazing at stepping back until I could pull myself together.

"Hey, are you all right?" my co-worker, Lorna asked as I made my way back toward my desk.

"Yeah, I'm okay. My allergies are acting up." I forced a smile.

Lorna shook her head as she noticed the stack of lottery tickets on my desk. "I see y'all still wasting your money on the devil's work."

I couldn't help but laugh at Lorna, who we called 'Oh Holy One' around the office. She was the self-appointed pointer-out of everything sinful but was the first person to bring you the latest office gossip.

"Come on, Lorna. If you win, you can give ten percent to the church," I said, managing a smile in her direction.

"Don't play with Jesus," she warned.

"Can you at least say a prayer that we win?" I asked.

"I'm going to pray for you all right," she said, shaking her head like I had a one-way ticket to hell.

We stopped talking as our coworker, my friend, Raquelle came marching across the room, her head bowed, her eyes puffy like she'd been crying as two security guards were flanked on both sides of her.

"What's going on?" I asked. I had just gotten her money for the lottery pool this morning and she seemed fine.

Raquelle didn't look up as they escorted her through our area. Her office in the finance department was in the back of the call center, so I assumed that was where they were going.

"Girl, you hadn't heard?" Lorna leaned over my cubicle and whispered.

"Heard what?" I asked.

"Word is that Raquelle apparently has been embezzling money from the company," Lorna whispered.

"Girl, shut up!" I exclaimed. I cupped my hands over my mouth and shook my head. I'd asked Raquelle if she had gotten a raise because she was shopping like I'd never seen her do before. Her job in the accounting department paid well, but the house she'd just moved into was much nicer than the one she'd lived in since I met her. And much more than I assumed she could afford on her salary. She was a single parent taking care of two kids, that's why I questioned the decision to buy such a lavish house. I never would've imagined that she was stealing.

Lorna was about to say something, but I ran over to Raquelle, who was standing outside her office as one of the guards went inside to retrieve her purse. "Raquelle, what's going on?"

My friend couldn't even make eye contact with me. She was shaking, like she was extremely scared. "I'll call you later," she said, her voice low.

Before I could say anything else, they whisked her away.

Chapter 4

Terrance

After work Sheray and I decided to grab a bite to eat at Cyclone Anaya's. The margaritas there were bangin'. And once we got married I found myself wired up and needing to take the edge off by having a drink. . . or three, more often than usual.

I turned into the parking lot and my mouth began to water when I thought about the cold, refreshing Tequila Gold I was about to enjoy. I'd become accustomed to meeting my buddies for a Friday happy hour every once in a while. But lately, I needed alcoholic beverages mid week.

Yes, I loved Sheray, as my girlfriend. I could send her home when she started working my nerves, or even make up an excuse to get away and just get my space. But as my wife, I was now stuck.

I grabbed the keys out of the ignition and glanced over at Sheray, who sat still with her hands on the straps of her purse. I reached for my door handle and when she didn't move, I frowned. "Umm. . . aren't you going to get out?"

"Yeah, I am, but I'm going to wait for you to come around and open the door for me," she said without even looking my way. "I was watching Steve Harvey and he said -"

I wasn't even up for the bull she was about to dish out. "Steve Harvey? Seriously? I don't care what anyone has to say. If you want me to open the door for you, then say that. Don't tell me what another man says, because that's the quickest way for me not to do it."

She finally looked at me, a cheesy grin spreading over her face. "Well, I was just thinking that since we're married now, we have to do things differently. You haven't been the most chivalrous man toward me, but now that I am your Missus that's gonna change."

She seemed proud of her statement. I would never understand why women thought putting on a ring and changing her last name would make a man think and act differently. If it were left up to me, we would have been dating for life. I shuddered as the words "Till death do us part" ran across my mind.

"What do you mean we need to do things different?" I asked. "I got something different for you. How about you stop watching all those damn talk shows and just be yourself."

I got out of the car, slammed the door, and proceeded to walk into the restaurant.

No sooner had I put our name on the waiting list for a table, I spotted my high school classmate, Veronica Walters standing at the bar. I didn't think it was possible, but she looked better than she did when we were in school. Nearly every male in the school wanted Veronica. She still had that bubble butt as we used to say. Her long, wavy hair was still long, though less wavy. She looked like she needed to be playing herself in a movie called "Fine and Finer."

Veronica's deep dimples popped as soon as she saw me. But before I could speak, Sheray waltzed in and locked hands with me. "How long is the wait, Baby?"

I wasn't surprised that Sheray came in pretending like we were the happiest couple on earth. Heaven forbid anybody thought we weren't.

"About fifteen minutes," I replied, my heart dropping as Veronica turned back to her friends at the bar.

"They have a lot of tables outside," Sheray said.

"I want to sit inside," I replied.

Either she didn't care about my attitude, or she was going to keep up her perfect façade, because she just said, "Okay, well I'm going to go to the ladies room and freshen up a bit." She pranced off, and I watched my wife's perfectly proportioned curvy body disappear around the corner.

A few minutes later, three quick taps on my shoulder startled me. I turned around and fought to contain my cool. "Hey, Veronica. What's been up?"

After flashing her bright smile, she said, "Nothing much." She looked me up and down. "Dang, ten years and you're still hot."

Me? I mean, I knew I wasn't some buster, but I would've never imagined Veronica had ever considered me hot.

She held her arms out. "Well, give me a hug."

I leaned in. Our hug probably lasted a bit longer than it should have but she felt, and smelled so good.

I inhaled. "Mmm. You smell amazing. And I don't have to tell you that you are still as stunning as I remember, because I'm sure you know that already."

"Ahem." Sheray stood with her arms crossed and her weight shifted to one side.

I stepped back and nervously said, "Sheray, this is one of my high school friends, Veronica. Veronica, this is. . ." I hesitated. This was my first time introducing Sheray as my wife.

"His wife, Sheray," she said, stepping up to shake Veronica's hand. I was definitely going to pay for that pause.

"Nice to meet you," Veronica said. She turned back to me. "Well, it was good seeing you, Terrance. You take care of yourself."

Sheray draped her arm through mine and flashed a fake smile. "That's what he has me for."

Veronica just smiled like she found the whole thing amusing. Me, on the other hand, I wanted to die.

"Take care, Veronica," I said as she walked away. Her hips swayed from side to side like a pendulum on a clock, and I felt myself drifting into a trance when Sheray elbowed me in the side.

"Really, Terrance?"

"Wh-what?" I stuttered.

"What was all that about?"

"What do you mean?"

"I heard you talking to her when I walked up. Don't play with me, Terrance."

"Okay, you're trippin' for real," I replied. "I hadn't seen the girl in ten years." I was grateful when the hostess walked up to show us to our seats.

I was hoping Sheray would let the whole thing with Veronica drop but of course, she wouldn't. As soon as we sat down, she went in.

"As your wife, you're going to have to respect me more."

"As a married man, you can't flirt with other women."

"Steve said. . . "

At that point, I tuned her out. The margaritas at Cyclone Anaya's were good at mellowing me out. So I ordered another one, then sipped away as my wife rambled on.

Chapter 5

Janine

I f I could find some way to kill my husband and get away with it, Lord knows I would. And believe me, I'd thought about it. From cyanide to carbon monoxide, to cutting his brakes, you name it, it had crossed my mind. But since I'd watched enough Lifetime to know that the woman always got caught, I pushed aside all thoughts of homicide and focused on keeping my tears at bay.

But as I watched my husband pack the last of his belongings, the tears betrayed me and broke free.

"So, just like that, you're gone?" I asked. I had been silently watching him pack for fifteen minutes.

"It's not *just like* anything," he replied. He closed his suitcase, then stood erect to face me. "We both know this has been a long time coming. I don't want to hurt you, but I'm tired of being unhappy."

I hated that Tony looked so good right now. I wanted him to be as ugly as he acted. But with his Idris Elba swag, and Shemar Moore looks, ugly could never be used to describe him.

"I've done everything I can to make you happy," I told him, struggling not to cry any more than I already was. "I cook, I clean, I screw you when you want to be screwed. I've done everything to be a good wife."

"Except be there for me."

"What are you talking about?" Tony hadn't really given me a reason for his unhappiness, except that he "just wasn't happy."

As if I couldn't feel any lower, his exasperated tone made me feel like a little girl getting on her father's nerves.

"Let's not make this any harder," he said. "Just let it go so we both can be happy."

I didn't know who this man was standing in front of me. We'd met when I was eighteen and working at Chili's Restaurant and he and his friends had come in after a basketball game. We'd immediately connected and since I'd been living with my aunt (my parents died when I was younger) he'd all but moved me into his apartment within two weeks. I got pregnant with our son and although we didn't get married immediately, he did marry me on William's first birthday. We'd built a decent life. It seemed like we never had enough money and I wanted more kids, but Tony was against it. But other than that, I would've never deemed us as "unhappy."

I couldn't figure out if Tony was going through a midlife crisis or if that little sleaze bucket had his nose wide open.

Then, Tony had the audacity to take my hand. "I didn't mean to hurt you and I hope that you can find it in your heart to one day forgive me."

I snatched my hand away. "What about William?"

"I'm always going to be there for my son."

"I don't want him around some bimbo," I snapped. That had been what I called her since I found out – via her sext messages to him – that they'd been having an affair for the past year. I'd gone digging through Tony's phone after the disastrous dinner, when he announced he wanted out. I wasn't normally a snooper, but I was trying to make sense of everything.

"See, that right there." Tony shook his head in frustration. "I'm not about to do any baby mama drama."

My mouth fell open. After giving him the best years of my life, I'd been reduced to a baby mama?

"Get out," I said, pushing him toward the door. "Get the hell out."

"And this is why men go to the other side."

I was just about to haul off and smack him when I saw my son standing there.

"Dad, you're leaving?"

I hurried to my son's side. "Baby, your dad -"

"And don't you badmouth me to him," Tony warned.

I turned and cut my eyes at him. Did he even know me? I couldn't stand him but I would never turn my son against his father.

"Honey, mom and dad are having some grown-up issues right now," I said, trying to sound reassuring.

"Is dad leaving?" he asked, staring at his father's suitcase.

"Just for a little while," I tried to sound comforting, but who was going to comfort me?

"Son, your mother and I are getting a divorce," Tony announced.

I stared at Tony in disbelief. We hadn't talked about telling our son that!

"Tony!" I snapped.

"What? It's no sense in sugarcoating anything," Tony said. "The boy has to learn to be a man. That's the problem, you're always babying him." He put his hand on William's shoulder. "Son, I'll never leave you, but your mother and I are over."

Hearing Tony say those words tore at my heart. I don't know why. I surely didn't expect us to stay married after he left me for that Pop Tart.

He continued, "But that has nothing to do with you. I will always be a part of your life."

William's eyes grew wide with panic. "Why, daddy? What did we do? Are you really leaving us?"

As tears began streaming down my son's face, my hatred for my husband deepened.

"I promise I'll be good, please don't leave." He reached for his father, but I pulled him back and into a hug. As my trembling son began sobbing like a baby, I gave Tony the eye to tell him if he knew what was best, he would get out now.

Tony leaned in and kissed our son on the head. "I love you and I'll be in touch."

And with that, he walked out of our lives.

I led my son out of our room and back into his.

"Mama, I don't understand. Why is daddy leaving?" William wiped his tears. He was trying to be a big boy, but I could tell it was killing him.

"Sometimes grown ups grow in different directions," I told him. "Your dad and I are just taking some time to figure things out. But know this, we both love you so much."

He looked at me with tear-filled eyes, like he didn't know what to believe. All I could do was take him into my arms.

I don't know how long we sat on his bed, me holding him tightly, but we both ended up dozing off. When I awoke, I eased him under the covers and made my way downstairs. It was almost eleven, so I needed to get ready for bed anyway. Shoot, I needed to get ready for the next chapter of my newly single life.

I had just turned off the lights in the kitchen when my front doorbell rang.

"What in the world?" I said. Who would be at my house that late at night? Maybe Tony had come to his senses. But then, why would he be ringing the doorbell? I glanced out the peephole and was shocked to see Angelique standing on the other side.

I swung the door open. "Angelique? What in the world are you doing here?"

She burst into my living room. "Are you alone?"

"William is upstairs sleep."

"Where's Tony?"

I sighed. "Long story. But he's not here. Why? What's going on?"

She was shaking so bad, I felt like she was on the verge of convulsing.

"Oh, my God. Oh, my God," she stammered.

"What? What is wrong?" I said. My heart had started pounding. "Did something happen with Marcus?"

Angelique reached in her bra and pulled out a little pink slip. "Look at this," she said, handing it to me.

I looked at it and said, "It's the lotto ticket. Okay, and?"

She thrust another piece of paper at me. "And look at this."

"What is this?" It looked like a printout of a website.

She tapped the paper. "It's the winning numbers from tonight's lotto."

"Okay."

"Look, look. They match!" she screamed.

It took a minute for it to register, then finally I said, "What?"

"We won! We won!" Angelique danced around my living room.

I looked at the ticket in my right hand, then the paper in my left. I did this two more times before staring at her. "We're millionaires?"

"We're millionaires!" Then, Angelique released a piercing scream loud enough to wake up the entire neighborhood.

Chapter 6

Angelique

I know it was crazy, but here it was midnight, and Janine and I were on our way over to Raquelle's. Our screams had awakened Janine's son and so we'd loaded him into the back seat and headed to Raquelle's to share the news. We had actually thought about waiting until morning, but both of us knew there was no way we'd be able to sleep. Marcus was working the overnight shift and couldn't be reached while he was in the field, so I'd have to wait until morning to tell him the good news.

Both Janine and I had called Raquelle and Terrance, but Terrance's phone was going straight to voicemail. There was no way I was going to call Sheray since she didn't even want him to play. We told Raquelle to hang tight as we were on our way over.

"I still can't believe this," Janine said, nervously bouncing her leg. "Our lives are about to change forever. We could go to any store we want and buy stuff without trying to figure out which bills we hadn't paid yet."

"Who are you telling?" I replied. "I know we play the lotto all of the time, but honestly, I never thought we would win."

Both of us smiled. The shock of everything was still setting in. We pulled into Raquelle's driveway, jumped out, and rang the doorbell over and over. I knew her kids were asleep, but I didn't let up on pressing the button. If they were awakened out of their sleep, I'm sure they would be happy to know that it was because they were rich. When I was young, I sure wouldn't have minded if someone had woken me up to give me some news like that.

Raquelle finally swung her door open, with a 'Who died?' look on her face.

"What in the world is going on?" she asked as we walked in. "I had just fallen asleep when y'all called. And after the day I've had. . . all I can say is this better be good." She rubbed her eyes and looked from me to Janine and back to me. Then, following a yawn, she said, "All right, one of you needs to start talking."

William dragged himself past us and over to her love seat, plopped down, and fell back asleep.

"Why do you have that baby out at this time of night?"Raquelle asked. And then she noticed the bottle in my hand. "And why do you have wine?"

I walked over to her and put my hands on her shoulders. "Okay, you need to sit down for this one."

"What's going on? Is one of you deathly ill? 'Cause if so, I can't take it." She massaged her temples. "I just can't take any more bad news."

Janine stepped toward her and said, "Girl, calm down. No one is gonna die. Not now anyway. And if they did, we could put them away nicely."

I giggled. "Really nice."

Raquelle squinted and held both hands up while she shrugged. "I'm lost and one of you better catch me up now or I'm gonna take myself back into my room and go to sleep."

"So here's the deal." I reached into my bosom and pulled out the piece of paper with the lotto numbers along with our ticket, and then I handed both to her.

Raquelle unfolded the ticket, did a quick scan of the numbers and the paper, then looked at us. "Is this what I think it is?"

Both Janine and I nodded in excitement.

"So, we're rich?" When we nodded again, she looked down at the ticket. "This has to be a joke." She turned the ticket over and looked at the fine print on the back like she was trying to make sure it wasn't some kind of prank. After a moment, her grin spread so wide that all of her teeth were visible. "We won?"

After another round of squealing and William whining that we "kept waking him up," we finally settled down.

"Can you believe it? You know we couldn't have called you with news like this. I'll bet you don't want to go back to sleep now, do ya?" Janine laughed as she sipped the Moscato I'd broken out in celebration.

Raquelle stared off and her smile faded. That made both me and Janine lose our smiles. How could she not be happy? "I have something to tell the two of you," she finally said.

Suddenly the room felt cold and stiff. I saw tears well up in my friend's eyes.

"What's wrong?" I asked. "Is this about what happened at work today?" I'd called her after work, but got her voicemail. I'd meant to call later in the evening, but then got sidetracked. "Lorna said something about you being fired."

She fidgeted, but didn't reply.

"You know you can tell us anything." I peered over and shot a curious look at Janine.

Raquelle took a deep breath. "I know I can tell you two anything, but this. . . " She shook her head. "I don't even know how to say it."

I rubbed her shoulder. "Just take your time and start from the beginning."

Raquelle was a model employee. I couldn't imagine what she had done to get fired. The longer it took for her to talk, the more anxious I got. And the Lord knows I didn't need to get nervous or anxious, because it only caused me to want a snack. Hunger had a way of sneaking up on me when I was nervous. If someone were to use my weight as an indicator of how nervous or afraid I'd been over the course of my life, they'd probably guess that I'd must have been scared all of the time. I refrained from walking into Raquelle's kitchen and rummaging through her pantry to find a late night snack to munch on while she discussed her situation with us.

Raquelle's chest lifted, then she blew a long breath before saying, "There is no easy way to put it, but ah, I might be going to jail."

"Jail?" Janine and I blurted out at the same time.

"Yes, you heard right." Raquelle looked down at the floor and allowed her long black hair to hide her face.

I couldn't see her face, but I could tell she was no longer teary eyed, she was crying.

"I stole money from the company," she confessed, before releasing an all-out sob.

It took a few minutes, but she finally calmed down enough to continue. She proceeded to explain how she took a little money here, then a little there until she got enough money for Shaun's medical bills.

"Then, I just got greedy," she admitted. "I'm such a horrible person." She paused as if a thought had just occurred to her. "Maybe I could use some of my winnings to pay him off."

"You're right," I said, snapping my fingers. "You're rich now. Having to pay back two hundred thousand dollars is not as tough when you are a millionaire."

We talked some more and I managed to cheer her up just enough for her to grin. "Go give Mr. Perry that money and move on with your life," I told her.

Raquelle looked hopeful as she raised her wine glass. "To new futures," she said.

"To better futures," I said.

Janine and I stayed with Raquelle a little longer, discussing how we'd tell Terrance tomorrow, then how we'd spend our money. Finally, around three a.m., we said our goodbyes.

"You girls are the best." Raquelle hugged us both, and when we got into my car, she closed the front door.

I leaned back against the seat, a smile across my face. My to-do list was ridiculous. I'd have to call the doctor first thing in the morning to book the one thing I wanted most in the world – my weight loss surgery. Then, I'd have to go to work and pretend like everything was normal. (I didn't know how long that would last).

Then I needed to find an attorney, because the three of us had already decided there'd be none of that publicly claiming our money at a press conference. But we'd set up a trust to claim the money. Of course, Terrance hadn't given his input, but we were sure he'd go along with us.

"What are you over there thinking about?" Janine asked me as I navigated the abandoned streets.

"How lucky we are," I replied.

"Honey, this ain't luck. We're blessed! I might just have to go back to church and tithe." She laughed.

"I know I am, even though I hadn't been since Easter of last year." We joked around some more until I pulled up in front of her house.

"Go try to get some sleep," I told her.

"Girl, I can't sleep. I need to know if anyone else won. Is the whole $62 million ours? So many questions. . . ."

"And we'll get our answers in due time." I motioned toward her sleeping son. "You need some help getting him inside? He's getting so big."

"Nah, I got him," she said, lifting William up like he was a toddler. She planted a kiss on his head. "I've been so excited about everything, I didn't tell you about Tony. But that's a story for another day. For now, I'm focusing on the positive and the life I'm about to build with my son."

I smiled at my friend. "See you tomorrow, I'm going home to wait for Marcus to get off work so I can tell him how our lives are about to change."

I was excited about all that was in store. I just had no idea how much things were actually about to change.

Chapter 7

Terrance

Thank God for different shifts. Sheray was still asleep when I ducked out this morning to head to work. She worked the 11-7 shift at Clearcast, but she always liked to get up and fix me breakfast before I left. But I didn't want breakfast. I wanted a break. I felt like I was being smothered. This sudden adjustment from bachelor to husband wasn't easy.

Sheray was always at my place, but she had officially moved in with me as soon as we got back from Vegas. She'd stopped at the post office and filled out a change of address on our way home from the airport. My bachelor pad became our home. I could tell already that working with Sheray as my wife wasn't going to be as fun and fulfilling as it was when we were dating. At first, I'd felt some kind of way about her transferring to my division, but I got over it. When we were dating, we'd take our lunch breaks together just to go to one of our places for a quickie. Sometimes we wouldn't make it past the car, and we didn't care. Sheray did anything for me when we were dating. After we said I do, she started giving me her list of don'ts. By the time we'd landed back in Houston, I felt like I had a checklist of things "that had to change."

Some of the expectations she had for me as a husband were impossible for me to meet. From the putting the toilet seat down every time to being home before ten p.m., Sheray had one requirement after another. I hadn't been married a week and Sheray had already turned into my mother, part two.

When we got home from Cyclone Anaya's, my wife proceeded to go in on me about how embarrassed she was when she walked up to me flirting with Veronica. And she didn't just say Veronica's name regularly, she rolled her neck and sang it with attitude. After listening to her ranting for thirty minutes straight, I grabbed a pillow and a blanket, then marched to the couch. This morning, my sore neck and shoulders were constant reminders that I didn't sleep on my Posturepedic mattress. But a sore neck and tense shoulders were more tolerable than a nagging woman.

Needless to say, my Thursday morning ride to work was nothing short of a much-needed respite.

Right before I turned into the parking lot, my cell phone rang. When I glanced at it and saw that it was Angelique for the fourth time since last night, I figured I should answer.

"What's up?"

"Hey, I just went by your cubicle. Where are you?"

"I'm pulling in now. What's goin' on?" I heard urgency in her voice. Now, I was nervous as I thought about the three missed calls last night from Janine as well. I hadn't answered any of the calls because I didn't want to give Sheray anything else to gripe about.

"Just meet me in the break room. I'll tell you everything once you get here," Angelique said.

Before I could press the End button, she added, "And hurry up."

I parked my car and gathered my ID badge, lunch, and work keys. When I arrived to the break room, Angelique and Janine were seated at the table where we normally ate lunch.

"Close the door," Angelique whispered.

I did as she said, then turned to both of them. "Okay, what's with this Top Secret stuff? Who died?"

They exchanged glances and the excitement in their eyes was the only thing that eased the jitters in my stomach. The way they were all lit up, meant no one we cared about had gone to the other side of the soil, as my mama used to say.

Angelique spoke first, a gigantic grin across her face. "You. Will. Never. Believe what we are about to tell you."

I slid into the seat across from them. "I wish you would stop playing games and just tell me. You're acting like you won the lott. . ." My words trailed off as Angelique slid two pieces of paper in front of me. One was a photocopy of a lottery ticket. The other was just a printout that said 'Tonight's Winning Numbers' at the top.

I wasn't comprehending the message my eyes were trying to send to my brain. "Does this mean what I think it means?" I asked.

"*We* won the lottery," Angelique said.

"Yep. We won. We are rich," Janine added, clapping her hands.

"Is this a joke?" I knew Janine could play around sometimes, but this was out of character for Angelique to play with my emotions like this.

"Boy, it's too early in the morning to be playing games," Janine said.

"And how long have you known me?" Angelique added. "You know I wouldn't play around with something like this."

My hands were trembling as I picked up both pieces of paper and compared the numbers. They were definitely a match. I even checked the dates to make sure they matched.

"Now from my understanding we have to contact the Texas Lottery Commission Headquarters in Austin," Angelique said. "Then, we have to set up an appointment to go there and claim our money."

"This is real?" I asked one more time just to be sure.

"As real as your marriage," Janine said with a grin.

My marriage. I was about to be a rich newlywed. I would've much rather been a rich bachelor.

"Okay, let's go," I said, standing up and grabbing my stuff.

"Go where?" Angelique asked.

I frowned. "Austin." That was a no brainer. In fact, they should've met me in the parking lot with this news so we could've hit I-10 immediately.

"Slow your roll," Angelique said, chuckling. "I want my money just like you, but financial rule 101 – we have to meet with a financial advisor first. I put in a couple of calls this morning and we have an advisor and an attorney that can meet with us after work."

"I don't need anyone to advise me of anything except which way to the lotto office," I replied.

"Do you want your name all out in the public?" Janine said.

"For real, you just gonna walk out with a check and go start spending?" Angelique added.

"Ummm, yeah," I said.

Angelique waved me off. "Boy, we have to be smart and strategic about this. That's the quickest way to end up broke."

I knew they were right, but I sighed anyway. "Fine, but are we all going to go talk to Evelyn together? Or did y'all want me to go first?" I looked at Janine and Angelique as I moved toward the break room door. Neither of them moved.

Angelique spoke before I exited. "Down, boy. I told you, we need to be smart about this. We don't know how many other people have tickets. For all we know, we could have to split this thirty ways, so let's not go telling Evelyn to screw herself just yet."

I stared at her. Leave it to Angelique to bust my planned triumphant revenge for that uptight Grinch, Evelyn. I had been promoted to a training coordinator, but she still treated me like I worked in janitorial services. I couldn't wait to tell her where to go. "Do you always have to be such a thinker?" I asked Angelique.

She shrugged. "Sorry, T. That's just the way I am." Then she joined Janine in a good laugh at my expense.

When the laughter died down, Angelique said, "You should have seen your face when you turned around. What were you going to do? Jump around yelling 'I quit' like they do on TV?"

I chuckled but didn't tell her that I'd planned to do the Cabbage Patch, the Running Man, and the Dougie on my way out the door. "Well, I guess it's no secret that when we do claim our money, I'll be quitting," I said.

Janine turned her lips up as she stood. "It's a good thing you didn't stick to the budget Sheray was hassling you about. Because if you would have, you would have been sick if we had won and you didn't. Shoot, you know Owen is gonna be pissed," Janine said.

"Too bad, so sad," Angelique replied.

"You guys don't think we should give Owen a cut?" Janine asked. "He did play with us a lot."

"But he didn't play this time," Terrance replied. "You can give him a cut of your portion since that's your boy, but he gets nothing from me!"

Owen and I used to be cool, but we'd been clashing lately, mainly because I'd gotten the promotion he'd wanted.

"Yeah, Janine," Angelique added. "We all agreed on the rules. You don't play, you don't win."

They could have this discussion all they wanted. I couldn't be worried about Owen. I was thinking about Sheray. Janine was right, if I had listened to my wife, I wouldn't have been able to even consider quitting my job. That thought led to another. Could I get my marriage annulled before we got the money? The thought that I'd have to give her fifty percent wasn't setting right with me. The way I saw it, if she didn't want to contribute to the pool, she shouldn't receive half of my winnings.

I decided that as soon as I got home, I would log on to my laptop and find out how to end my marriage.

"All right, ladies. Since y'all won't let me quit yet, I'd better get to work. I'll see you all later." I walked out of the door and had just turned the corner when I bumped right into Sheray.

"Good morning, Hubby." She bounced up and kissed me on the cheek like we hadn't slept apart last night. "I just love how that sounds."

Choosing to ignore her last comment, I said, "Why are you here so early?"

"I came to talk to Evelyn about moving my shift. It really doesn't make sense that we work two different shifts. If we work the same time, then we can come to work together."

It took everything inside me to suppress my groan. I probably should've told her about the wonderful news I'd just received, but if she was acting like this now, I could only imagine how she'd act once she found out I was rich.

"Well, I gotta go ahead and get to work. Have a great day." I kissed her forehead, only because she was going for my lips, then found my way to the elevator. I drew in a deep breath and shook my head knowing that I had to find an escape from her or I was going to smother from her overbearing love.

Chapter 8

Raquelle

It had been less than twenty-four hours since my life got turned upside down. I couldn't even muster up enough joy to be excited about the winning lottery ticket because I envisioned myself locked up in a cell, wishing I could spend the money.

I rocked in my recliner as I sipped my morning cup of coffee. Tiana and Shaun had left for school and to my surprise, neither of them asked why I was still in my robe when they left. There were many mornings I'd get up for work and wish I could stay in my robe and relax all day. That's why you have to be careful what you wish for.

Winning the lottery was great, but I didn't have a clue as to how long it would take before I could get my hands on the money. Right now, though, my focus was on staying out of jail. The first order of business was for me to consult an attorney, and a very good one. I wanted to call Mr. Perry and tell him I really could pay the money back. . . with interest. But, after searching the

Internet, I learned that it wasn't as easy as that. Still, I didn't think it would hurt to try, but I wanted to do so under the advice of an attorney. I didn't need bribery being added to the charges already being pressed against me.

I picked up my cell phone and dialed the number of a lawyer I'd found on the Internet.

I left a message for the attorney to call me, throwing in that I'd won the lottery so he'd call me back quicker. Just as I placed my phone back on the kitchen counter, it rang again. I recognized it was the number to Shaun's Nephrologist's office.

"Hello?"

I was met with a chipper voice. "Good morning, Mrs. Vargas, this is Tami, the nurse, from Dr. Newsome's office. How are you?"

"Oh hi, Tami. I'm good. How about yourself?" It always had amazed me that no matter what was going on in a person's life, when they're asked how they're doing, most people replied that they are doing well.

"I'm well. I think you're going to be even better once I give you some information regarding Shaun's transplant."

"I'm sure I will. Anything positive about this will ease my mind." Watching my son go through this was the most difficult thing of my life. Anything that could alleviate that pain was welcomed news.

"We have a donor! They can't do it until April because of some type of religious reason, but isn't that awesome news?"

Before I knew it, I blurted out, "April? Are you kidding me? April? It's only February. My baby needs a new kidney and the best they can give me is two months?" I knew that I should be grateful that he had a donor, but the mother in me didn't want my son suffering one day longer than he had to.

"Well, Mrs. Vargas, Shaun is a very blessed little boy. The person that is donating their kidney is doing so because of the post they saw on Facebook asking people for donations to a fund for Shaun. There are over 100,000 people in the United States that have been waiting for an organ for years. Shaun is getting his in two months." Then, she paused. "I know this is a difficult time for you and your family. I was hoping to make your day a little brighter by giving you the news, but it seems as though I did just the opposite."

I took a deep breath and closed my eyes. "No, it's not your fault. I am grateful. I just want my son to get better. Thanks for calling. Let me know what I need to do from here."

"I can only imagine what you're going through. No parent ever wants to see their child hurt, especially when there's nothing we can do to make them better. When Shaun comes in for his next appointment, Dr. Newsome will explain everything you need to know regarding the procedure and things you can do to prepare for it."

She gave me the info for his follow up appointment. "Thanks, Tami. Have a great day."

"You too, Mrs. Vargas."

When we hung up, I rested my head in my recliner and rocked back and forth. In one day, so many things had changed in my life: I'd lost my job, was on the verge of getting arrested, won the lottery, and my son got a kidney donor. The latter two things should cancel out everything else. That thought made me smile for the first time in days.

Chapter 9

Janine

I should have known that trying to stay at work after I found out we won the lottery was going to be difficult.

When we first started doing the office pool, me, Owen and Terrance used to imagine the different ways we would quit. So having to wait was killing me.

We had found out yesterday that we were the sole winners and would be taking home thirty-five million after taxes since Angelique had opted for the cash payout. Divided four ways, that was almost eight million each once the attorney and financial advisor Angelique had hired got their cut. We'd met with them last night for almost four hours. Raquelle wasn't as happy as the rest of us, because they said she'd need a criminal attorney for her case, so she was distracted all evening. But me, Angelique and Terrance were floating high. Eight mil was a nice little come up. I couldn't retire indefinitely, but I sure could relax a while, maybe even go to

Cosmetology school and open my own salon, a dream I had long ago given up.

We'd worked out all the logistics and the JART Trust would claim our winnings on Monday. It was only a couple of days, but I knew that waiting until Monday was going to be pure hell for me. The minutes leading up to me getting that money in my hands couldn't have ticked away any slower.

The first thing I planned on doing was getting a new home for me and William because the mere thought of staying in the same home that Tony and I shared made me nauseous. I hadn't slept well since he made his announcement that our life together was really over. I came home from the meeting last night and everything that belonged to him was gone. Not a trace of him was left except for our family photos. That bastard wasted no time in cleaning house.

"Are you all right?" Angelique stood inside of my cubicle squinting at me with her hands on her hips.

"Yeah, I'm fine. Why?"

"Well, I called your name three times and you never responded. You look like you were in a daze. I hope you're not contemplating quitting." We had wanted to be strategic in our exit since we really weren't trying to have folks in our business. Raquelle was already gone, but we'd agreed that Terrance would quit today, I would call Monday and quit, and Angelique – since she could tolerate this place more than any of us – would work an extra week and not quit until next Friday. How she would be able to do that was beyond me.

"No, I'm sticking to the plan," I said.

She shook her head and kept her eyes on me as she spoke slowly. "Well then, what's wrong with you? Is it Tony, are you ready to tell me what happened?" Angelique had asked me about Tony a couple of times but I simply hadn't been ready to talk about it.

I sighed, deciding to finally tell her everything. I started from the beginning, and finished with, "I just can't get over the fact that Tony left me. I have about eight minutes to get myself together so I can start taking phone calls and I can't even concentrate."

Angelique put her hand on my shoulder. "It's gonna be okay. I know it sucks even more for you knowing that he's gonna get half of your lottery earnings. That sure would piss me off. I mean just think he -"

I held my hand up, and didn't care that I cut her off. "Hold up. Half of my earnings? Oh no he won't. He left me before I won, so when he left me, he lost his chances to get half of *my* money."

My friend shook her head. "It doesn't work like that. You are still married and by right he is entitled to fifty percent of everything you guys have accumulated while being married."

"The devil is a lie!" I knew I'd have to look into it, but I would fight for every penny of my money if I needed to. I looked at the clock on the corner of my computer and saw that I had three minutes before calls would start rolling in. I slipped my headphones on as a signal to Angelique that I was finished with our conversation. She took the hint and walked away, knowing that she, too, had calls to take.

I pressed the light to answer the switchboard. I'd gotten written up for that last customer I cussed out, so I'd promised Evelyn I was going to try and have a better attitude. Of course, that promise was made before I became a millionaire. Even still, I plastered on a smile and said, "Good morning, thanks for calling Clearcast, this is Janine. How may I assist you today?"

"Look, Janet, my cable bill is way too high. I need you to do something about it, 'cause I'll starve before I pay two hundred and fifteen dollars for some cable."

"My name is Janine. But I would be happy to pull up your account if you can verify some information for me. Who am I speaking with?"

"This is Beautiful Jakes. Now can you hurry and check my account. I have to go to work in a few minutes and I need to know what my balance is."

I paused. "Beautiful?"

"That's my name!" she said.

"Like, that's what your mother named you?" I couldn't help but ask, as I envisioned this hideous looking woman.

"Look, you don't need to worry about all that. Just hurry your ass up."

Woosah. . . "Yes, ma'am, Ms. Jakes. I'm going to go as fast as I can. Would you mind giving me the last four digits of the account holder's social security number?"

She had obviously transitioned from home into her car for her commute to work, because all of a sudden the radio was blasting in my ear. It was so loud I could barely make out the words as she spoke.

"I apologize, Ms. Jakes, I couldn't understand the numbers you just called out. Would you mind repeating them?"

She huffed and said, "Look, I don't have time to play with you. You people at this company are so incompetent. Every time I call, there's a problem."

This lady was really testing my patience, but I decided to stay calm and use my best customer service skills. "I just couldn't hear you over the radio. Would you mind turning it down just a little then repeating your response?"

"Yes, I mind. How dare you ask me to turn down my radio? I want to speak to your manager. You have been rude to me since we began this phone call. If you don't like what you do, then you should get an education so you don't have to work in menial positions."

I didn't know where Ms. Jakes got off talking to me like she did, but she had another thing coming if she thought I was going to stand for that. Granted, I hadn't been to college, but that was beside the point. "You're right, Ms. Jakes. I think I'll go ahead and register for my classes as soon as I hang up this phone." I disconnected the call, removed my headphones, and picked up my purse. I'd tried to hold out and not quit until I had my money in my hands, but I'd had enough of rude customers.

I marched right over to Evelyn's office. Angelique was just going to have to be mad. Plan A had just shifted to Plan B. "Yo, Evelyn, this is my last day. I quit."

I tossed my headset on her desk, turned around and walked off. I'd never felt more exhilarated.

When I got into my car, I pulled out my sunglasses and drove out of the parking lot. After discovering that there was a possibility that Tony could get some of my money, it was like everything had become a blur. There was no way I was going to let that man lay so much as a fingernail on my money.

Chapter 10

Angelique

Today was a good day. Everything was all set for us to head to Austin tomorrow and my boyfriend and I had just had what he called our "last homemade meal for a while because we were going to eat out daily now that we were rich."

It didn't bother me that he automatically started talking about "us" being rich. Marcus had moved in with me three years ago to help me with the bills and had ended up taking over my rent altogether. He did everything for me and I couldn't imagine not sharing in this windfall with him. Marcus and I had an amazing relationship. He was loving, doting, and supportive, so he was right, *we* were going to have fun spending this money.

I set his wine glass down on the table in front of him.

"Now, we're ready to eat," I said, smiling at him.

"Baby, you're doing such a great job with your clean eating. I know it hasn't been easy, but we are in this together," he said as he surveyed the marinated chicken breast and salad that I had prepared. He pulled me down on his lap and snuggled in my bosom. I hated when he did that. I was sure that every time he hugged or squeezed me he was just as disgusted with my weight as I was, but he'd never tell me. Marcus was so sweet; he never acted as if my weight repulsed him. When we made love I always insisted that we do it with the lights off or I'd keep my top on. He knew that was the rule and he never pressured me to do anything different. He complimented me a lot and told me that he didn't care what I looked like with my clothes off because he loved me unconditionally. While all of that may have been true, it didn't change the fact that I didn't like how I looked naked.

Feeling the need to get him distracted from my rolls and plush body, I released myself from his embrace and sat down across from him.

"I can't wait until tomorrow," I said. "I just can't believe this time tomorrow, our lives will change so drastically."

"Babe, I'm so happy for you. For us. You know how bad I've been wanting to go to Aruba. I want that to be one of the first things that we do."

I cringed. "Umm, yeah, not so fast. You know I'm not going anywhere near a beach until after my surgery."

That wiped the smile off his face. "What?"

I knew that Marcus was against my surgery, but this wasn't open for discussion.

"Yep, it's amazing what money can do. Dr. Taylor has me scheduled for Thursday after next," I said. "It's an outpatient surgery, so I don't even have to stay overnight."

"Are you serious?" he replied. "I thought you had to go through months of therapy, and nutrition classes."

"You have to do all that when you're trying to get your insurance to cover it. When you're paying cold, hard cash, you set your date and go."

Marcus set his fork down and leaned back in his chair. "I keep telling you, you are beautiful just as you are. You don't need gastric bypass surgery."

"And I keep telling you, not only do I need it, I want it. More than I've ever wanted anything in my life." I didn't want to have this serious conversation on the eve of such a life-changing event, but we might as well get it out of the way, because I would be going under the knife come Thursday.

"Why can't you see what I see?" he asked.

I sighed. I wish I could see what Marcus saw. But since he was the only one who did see the beauty, I had to assume it was something wrong with his eyesight.

"Marcus, I don't expect you to understand. All my life, I've been the big girl. My father made disparaging remarks. My mother made excuses. One time, when I was thirteen, I was at a birthday party, stuffing my face with cake like every other kid there and this woman looked at me with such disgust, my mother stepped in and I just knew she was about to go off on that woman. Instead she said, 'She has a thyroid problem.' Do you know how much that hurt me?"

"I understand that," Marcus said. "But both of your parents have been deceased for years. You can't continue to carry the burden they put on you."

I struggled not to cry. "Don't you get it, this isn't about them. It's about me. It wasn't just them. It was friends, family, the person at the store, walking down the street. Everyone looked at me with pity and disgust."

"You're on the right path. You've lost four pounds."

I swear I wanted to throw my chicken breast at him.

"I'm sorry," he said when he saw the glare on my face. "I'm just saying that's progress. It's something to be proud of."

"Do you want me to stay fat so no one else will want me? That's what you want, huh?"

He stared at me, stunned. "I can't believe you would say that."

I glanced at my plate as I stabbed my spinach like it was his head. "I guess the truth hurts."

"You know, I would get mad at that," he finally said, "but I know you know better." He got up and moved toward me. "If the surgery is what you want to do for you, so you can feel better about yourself, then fine. I'm just saying, I think you're beautiful just as you are." He pulled me up and out of my seat.

I relaxed. I could never stay mad at Marcus. And what did I look like getting mad at someone who was just trying to love me as I was?

"Admit it, you'd love to see me prance around the bedroom in some itsy bitsy lingerie," I joked as he took me into his arms.

"Nah, I prefer to see you prance around the room in your birthday suit."

"You know that's not going to happen." I kissed him. "Maybe after my surgery."

He shook his head as he hugged me tighter. No, Marcus didn't get it. But he would soon see, when I was a hundred pounds lighter, he'd agree – surgery was the best decision I could have ever made.

Chapter 11

Terrance

I never claimed to be perfect. I never even wanted anyone else to think I was. Making mistakes was a part of life, and getting married was one mistake I could get a do-over for. Don't get me wrong; being married to Sheray wasn't torturous because of her. It was all me. I was to blame for my discontent. I'd done something I never should've done: Said 'I do.' Shoot, I was still working on my willingness to wear my wedding ring for the seven days we'd been married.

I never understood why wearing a piece of jewelry was so important to some people. . . especially women. Sheray didn't waste any time dragging me to a jewelry store in Vegas so I could buy her a ring so we could "properly exchange vows." We couldn't afford much more than a solid gold band for both of us. The other option was for her to get a small wedding set and I get nothing. She wasn't having that. So, we settled for the wedding bands. I know I was buzzing from the liquor because even as we tried on the rings, it didn't completely register what was about to happen. In fact, I remember leaving the ring store and Sheray saying we were going to a chapel, but everything after that was a blur.

I still hadn't told Sheray about the lottery, but since we were going to claim the money tomorrow, I couldn't put it off any longer. She had come home asking if I'd heard that some people in the building had won. Our building was huge and heavily staffed, so unless people worked in close proximity to one another, it was difficult to know what was going on throughout the entire company. I'd made up some excuse and left the room without answering her.

From the moment we returned from Vegas, I'd considered getting an annulment. Now the thought of the lifestyle winning the lotto would bring me, made me want my single life back even more. But the good guy inside me won out, and I decided to tell her over dinner tonight. Since the money was won during our marriage, Sheray was entitled to fifty percent of my earnings no matter how quickly our marriage was dissolved.

I'd told Sheray not to cook because I was taking her out to dinner. She immediately started in about "watching our budget" but I just tuned her out.

By the time we pulled into Pappadeaux, our favorite seafood restaurant, Sheray was over any budget concerns and seemed thrilled to be going out. She sashayed to the door and smiled as she stood waiting for me to open it.

"Thank you, Baby." She walked in and slid her arm in mine. The one deep dimple she had appeared in her left cheek.

"My pleasure." My wife was beautiful and carried herself like a lady and I actually hoped her half of the money could bring her some joy. I took a deep breath as we walked up to the hostess to put our name on the waiting list.

"There's a thirty minute wait," the young hostess said as she handed me a buzzer.

Sheray and I headed to the bar and ordered some drinks.

All of a sudden I felt a strong tug on my shoulder. "What's up, Terrance? How's it goin'?" It was Owen.

"Everything's going well. I can't complain."

"Hey, Owen," Sheray said. Her cheerful personality could warm up the coldest room.

"Hey, Pretty Lady."

They hugged, and then Owen said something that changed my whole night. "Word is, our lotto pool hit."

My mouth dropped open in disbelief. How in the world did he know? I couldn't believe Janine or Angelique had said anything. I hadn't talked to Raquelle, but I couldn't believe she'd say anything either.

"Wh-what? Where did you hear that?" I stammered as Sheray's eyes bore into me.

"Lorna from the office said she overheard Angelique and Janine talking. Then Janine quit on Friday."

Janine quitting had thrown Angelique into a tizzy. She'd texted me telling me I couldn't quit yet, so as far as anyone knew, I was still a Clearcast employee.

Owen narrowed his eyes, like he was studying me. "So what's up? Did *we* win?"

If my wife hadn't been there throwing daggers at me, I would've busted out laughing.

"You need to check your sources, dude," I managed to say just as our buzzer went off. "That's our table." I took Sheray's arm. "See you at work tomorrow."

I know I was trembling as I walked away, but I tried my best to play it cool.

The hostess directed us to our booth and as soon as we both were seated, Sheray folded her arms. "Did you win?" she asked me point-blank.

I sighed heavily. I was in a no-win situation now. "Actually, that's why I brought you to dinner. To tell you the good news."

She cocked her head. "So please help me understand how the office gossip pool knows about this win before your wife?"

"I have no idea," I confessed. "Me, Angelique and Raquelle hadn't told anyone."

She shook her head in disbelief. "Including me." She grabbed her purse and scooted out of the booth. "I've suddenly lost my appetite," she said, heading toward the door.

I followed Sheray out to the car. I could barely keep up. By the time I got to the driver's side, she was sitting in the passenger seat with her arms folded, her gaze fixated straight ahead of her. "Start explaining now."

"You don't want to come in and discuss this over dinner?"

She glared at me so hard, I was momentarily speechless. "I know what you're thinking. . . " I finally began.

"I doubt that." Her lips were clinched tight.

"I was gonna tell you that we won over dinner."

"There is no way you didn't know you won. The word has been buzzing around the office all day Friday. I even mentioned it to you and you didn't say a word. I just never put it all together."

I swallowed hard as I thought of a good enough reason to tell my wife why I hadn't told her we were millionaires. "I was gonna surprise you."

"What a bunch of crap, Terrance. You are such a liar. Why did I have to find out from someone that heard it through the grapevine?" When she finally looked at me with tear-filled eyes, I could see the hurt and betrayal she felt. "Take me home."

I reached over and touched her lap.

She moved my hand. "Don't. You. Touch. Me."

I knew she meant business when I saw her elevated right eyebrow. Then, she folded her arms.

"I was gonna tell you, but. . ."

"You have yet to see what you have in me as a woman," she said. "You don't appreciate me. I try to make things between us great. I have ignored so many of your flaws and your rude actions. What did you think I would do if I found out about the money? Spend it all on myself? Go out and buy a yacht? What?" She held her hands out as she waited for my response.

"To be honest, I don't know why I didn't tell you when I found out." I shook my head. "I really don't. Maybe I was being selfish. I'm not used to being married." I stopped talking before I dug myself into an even bigger hole. When I looked over at Sheray, she had her hand by her nose and she was shaking her head as tears trickled down her cheeks.

"All I have done is try to be the best wife I know how to be, and this is the payback I get? Take me home. I am going to pack a few things and go back to my place

---

until the realtor sells it. You go ahead and stay with your money." She paused. "I didn't care whether we had two dollars or two million, I love you. I don't care about material things. Just thinking about you keeping something like that from me disgusts me and makes me question who you even are."

Seeing Sheray hurt didn't make me feel good, but maybe it was best that she moved out. I felt relieved because she made the suggestion about her leaving, not me. I started the engine and we drove home in silence.

Chapter 12

Janine

As the clock ticked toward ten p.m., I found myself doing something I hadn't done in six years. I never thought I'd touch another cigarette, let alone find myself puffing on three in a row. When Tony decided to leave me for his lil' girlfriend, that should have been enough to cancel his chances of receiving any of my lottery winnings. But as it turned out, he was not only entitled to get some of the money, he was eligible to receive half. After finding that out, I figured smoking a pack of cigarettes was better than plotting a murder.

"Mom, what are you doin' smoking a cigarette?"

William knew how I felt about him staying up too late on a school night. I tapped my cigarette twice on the edge of my ashtray and looked at my son. "I have a lot on my mind. And, anyway, I'm grown. I ask the questions here." I laughed. "Why are you out of bed?"

William walked over to the kitchen table where I was seated. "I can't sleep. Why isn't dad coming back? What did you do to him?"

Before I could speak I swallowed hard. I wasn't expecting my ten-year-old son to ask me that type of question. I felt my brows furrow as I stared into my son's teary eyes. "Honey, what makes you think I did something to your father?"

"Because he just left and never came back. Dad would never do anything like that." He put his head down and dried his tears by wiping his face on his shoulder. Tony and I raised William to know that it was okay for a male to cry. Even though he knew I wouldn't reprimand him for crying, I could tell he was trying his best not to break down.

"Yeah, that's what I thought too, but. . . " At that point, I had to pause in order to gather my thoughts. I had a tendency to say whatever came to mind without any regard to anything or anyone around me. But when it came to William, my instincts were to protect him from anything that could cause him pain. Rather than telling him what a jerk his father was, I opted to take the high road and be mature with my response. "Well, sometimes things happen and we may never learn why. But what I can tell you is that I did not do anything to your father to make him leave."

His eyes became brighter with a glimpse of hope. "So, do you think he's gonna come back?"

I grabbed William and pulled him close to me. "Of course he will come by to see you and you two will spend lots of time together." I swallowed hard to get the lump out of my throat. My son was visibly hurt, and there was nothing I could do to ease his pain. Of course, I could've told him that we were now rich, but I couldn't trust a child who loved his no-good daddy with that kind of information.

"I mean, do you think he is going to come back and live with us?"

Hell, no was what I wanted to say, but again, I had to play nice for the sake of my son's feelings. "No, he won't be coming back to live with us, but just because he won't live in the same house as you doesn't mean he loves you any less."

For the first time in William's life, I did question Tony's love for him. I could not understand how Tony could look at his reflection in the mirror and not see a man who tore his son's world apart.

Before Tony announced that he was leaving, our marriage was solid, so I thought. Maybe I was naïve when I believed all the late nights he claimed he was out with the boys.

"I miss daddy so bad," William said.

"I know. It's just different without him being here. But we still have each other."

I could see the hurt on his face as he kissed me on the cheek and said, "Goodnight, Mom." He'd had enough of our conversation and I understood that I shouldn't force him to talk.

"Goodnight, Baby. Anytime, you want to talk I'm here. And don't forget, you're going home with Jacob tomorrow. I've packed your bag. His mom will make sure you get to school Tuesday and I'll be back by the time you get home from school."

Normally, the idea of spending the night with his best friend, Jacob would send him over the edge with excitement, but my son just nodded as he sulked back to his room.

I contemplated taking another drag of my cigarette, but I was no longer confident that it would help calm my nerves. I felt a single tear trickle down my cheek. The tear wasn't because I was sad. I empathized with my son because our family life was stripped from him and there was nothing he could do about it. Tony's selfishness had caused more heartache than he could have imagined. It was one thing to hurt me, but his absence was tearing my son apart and I wasn't going to stand for it.

I picked up my cell phone and dialed Tony's number.

"Hello?"

I started speaking without giving any regard to him possibly being busy. He didn't care about disrupting my life when he announced that he was leaving me for another woman. "Tony, we need to talk. What you've done to our family isn't cool. Our son needs you, and he thinks that our split is because of something I did. You need to fix it."

I crossed my legs and I could feel my face turning red. I had one eyebrow raised. When I realized the scowl I had on my face, I relaxed because it wasn't like he could see me anyway.

"Look, Janine. I was sort of in the middle of something. I would be more than happy to talk to you tomorrow."

"You're in the middle of something or in the middle of *someone*?" I stopped myself before I ended up saying more than I needed to. "You know what? Forget I even called." I hung up before he got a chance to speak.

I hit my hand on the kitchen table causing a few of the ashes from the ashtray to fly up and land on the table. "Damn you, Tony," I muttered. And now, his bad behavior was about to be rewarded with half my money.

As I sat there, fuming, an idea suddenly popped into my head. I picked up my cell phone and called my cousin, Darnell. He wasn't the most tactful person in the world, but I knew I could trust him. We grew up together, like brother and sister, since his mother, my Aunt Ora raised me after my parents were killed in a car accident when I was twelve.

Darnell picked up on the first ring. "Yo, what up, cuz?"

"Hey, D. Did I catch you at a bad time? I need to talk to you about something important."

"Naw, I'm just headed home from work. What's goin' on? You need me to slide by?" Darnell was three years younger than me but the way he protected me, no one could ever tell. He worked as a deliveryman for a local furniture store. I knew he was struggling to make ends meet, and I figured our deal would help him tremendously.

"No, we can talk now," I said. "Are you alone?"

"Yes, ma'am. I'm about to roll by LaQuanta's crib. But, I'm all ears. If this is something about Tony, you know I got your back, cuz. Mama told me he left you for a teenager. Pervert. Just say the word and I'll handle him. The way he just left you hanging like that really - "

"No, it's not about Tony," I said. I had to cut him off because if I didn't there was no telling what he would say and I certainly didn't need any more motivation to be upset with Tony. "Well, it is, but not like you're thinking. I need you to do me a favor."

"Oh. . . all right. Whatcha need?"

"I have some news. But I need to swear you to secrecy." We were from a pretty big family, but our family was loud, dysfunctional, and full of moochers. The last thing I wanted anyone knowing was I'd come into any amount of money.

"Okay, this sounds serious. What's up?"

I inhaled, hoping that I was doing the right thing. "I won some money."

"Word? At the Casino?"

"No. The lottery." I paused. "I'm part of a pool that is splitting sixty-two million. I mean, we'll probably only get about half that after Uncle Sam gets his cut, but still."

Silence filled the phone. Finally, Darnell said, "Why you on my phone playing games with me, Janine?"

That made me laugh. Why did everyone think it was a joke when I said we'd won the lottery? "I'm not playing, lil' cousin. This is real. Very real."

I heard the music in the background cut off and it sounded like he had stopped his car.

"I had to pull over because I know I did not just hear you say you won sixty-two million dollars?"

"It's not going to be that much after taxes. And then I'm splitting it four ways. So when all is said and done, I'm only getting a little under eight million."

"Eight million dollars!" he screamed.

"Yes, and that's where I need you."

"You need me to help you spend it," he said, excitedly.

I laughed. "Not really. I need you to help me claim it." I proceeded to explain to him how Tony was entitled to half and it would be a cold day in hell before I let that happen. "We're claiming it through a trust, but all members of the trust have to be present to claim the winnings. Even though it's supposed to be private and our names aren't supposed to be released, it is reported to the IRS, which means that Tony can find out about it."

"Shoot, you know I don't care about Uncle Sam. I'm using a fake social security number anyway."

I shook my head at my cousin. Only he would go to work every day under somebody else's social security number.

"Well, I'll give you a cut for helping me out. I figured it would help you out and that way, I can keep Tony from getting any portion of my money."

"When you need me to do it?" That's what I loved about my cousin. He didn't need any more details.

"Tomorrow. I know it's last minute, but I just thought of the idea."

"Hey, you know I got your back. I'm off tomorrow anyway. Even if I weren't, I'd make a way to help you. That dude don't deserve one penny of your money."

"Awesome. I'll get you a flight out. We're all going at nine in the morning."

"You're going?"

"I'm going to Austin, but I'll have to stay in the hotel room. I can't chance anyone taking pictures, but I need to be there when y'all come back with the check."

"I know that's right. I know you won with your coworkers, but you can't trust folks these days."

I smiled. Darnell was always looking out for me. "They're good people. I trust them. But I wanna be there anyway."

"Cool." He actually let out a yell. "Dang. We 'bout to get paid."

"Yes, we are," I said. I hadn't decided how much I'd give Darnell, but he was small time. I'd slide him two or three hundred thousand dollars and I'd make his life.

"I really appreciate you, Darnell. This means so much to me," I said.

We said our goodbyes and I picked up my ashtray and walked over and dumped it and the remaining cigarettes into the trash. I wouldn't need them anymore. I was about to be stress-free.

Tony didn't know it yet, but he did me and my bank account a favor by walking out on our marriage.

Two Months Later...

Chapter 13

Raquelle

"Yes, I'll hold. . . again." I rolled my eyes up as the receptionist at Haskell and Haskell Law Firm placed me on hold for the third time in less than ten minutes.

My criminal attorney, Robert Haskell was in the process of negotiating a plea deal with Mr. Perry. Two months ago, he'd informed my former boss that I had won the lottery and would be willing to pay back triple the amount I took. We both thought that was more than generous and I had been praying that Mr. Perry would take us up on our offer. And since I hadn't heard back from Mr. Haskell, I was following up myself.

"Mrs. Vargas, are you still on the line?"

"Yes, I'm still here." I squinted and shook my head. Where else did she think I'd be? "What did he say?"

"Well, I am not at liberty to discuss the details of your case, but I can put you through to Carla if you'd like," she said, referring to Mr. Haskell's legal assistant.

"Pauline, with all due respect, I have been on this phone with you for the past ten minutes, I'm tired of getting the run around," I said.

I couldn't understand why I'd been put on hold several times for Mr. Haskell if she knew she couldn't help me. I should have known to ask for Carla, who I dealt with directly on a regular basis anyway. Mr. Haskell only got directly involved when it was time to go to court, which we'd done a month after I was fired, begging for an extension on a hearing so I could deal with my son. Mr. Haskell was the best criminal defense attorney in the Houston area and he'd managed to get everything delayed until after Shaun's kidney transplant. So it really didn't matter to me how much he interacted with me. What mattered to me was that he would see to it that I didn't get put behind bars.

Shaun's kidney transplant was scheduled for three weeks from now and now that we had a date set for that, we'd received notice yesterday that Mr. Perry would be pressing the district attorney for a court date.

I couldn't go to jail. I needed to be free for my children and if it took me spending every bit of my money to do it, I would.

Finally, Carla picked up the phone. "Mrs. Vargas. How are you?"

I could hear apprehension in her voice. "I'm all right, Carla. How about yourself?"

"Well, I'm doing good. I could be better though."

I could tell her news wasn't going to be good.

"Unfortunately, Mr. Perry is not willing to accept our offer," she continued. "He says that no amount of money can make this okay. A court date has been set for five weeks from today. I'm really sorry about all of this."

I had to steady myself against the staircase. "Oh-kay. Thank you, Carla. I have to go." I hung up the phone before I had a bonafide breakdown.

Though I didn't want to face it, the harsh reality was that the decisions I made would have several negative repercussions on my children.

No. This was not the end. It couldn't be. I would talk to Mr. Perry myself. The last time we talked, he was angry. I'm sure he'd settled down by now. And he knew, despite what I'd done, I'd been a good employee before that. In fact, his old behind used to flirt with me all the time.

I didn't care what lengths I had to go to in order to get Mr. Perry to take our offer. I was sure I'd have to give up more than the money, but I was willing to give Mr. Perry anything he wanted. . . and I do mean anything.

Chapter 14

Angelique

I t had been eight weeks since my surgery and I'd already dropped sixty pounds. Even though Marcus was upset that I had my surgery two days after my check cleared the bank, he'd been right by my side and no words could express my gratitude for him. He didn't know, but I'd paid Dr. Taylor extra just to expedite things. That was my first dose of how money really did change things. I'd had liposuction to get rid of the excess skin one month after the surgery. Dr. Taylor wanted me to wait because he said I'd lose more weight but what good was losing all that weight if I still didn't look good naked? Of course, once again, money talked and he'd done the lipo and I planned to go back as many times as necessary until my body looked like it was perfectly sculpted by Michelangelo himself.

I'd just left another appointment and Dr. Taylor had cleared me to resume my regular activities. His suggestion was that I not overexert myself and to listen to my body because it would let me know when I'd done too much. When I pulled out of the parking lot, my new body told me to head to the mall. I'd been holding off on shopping because I was determined not to buy any clothes until I could get them in a size ten. And that ten was calling my name! I was floating high and my debit card was ready to hit the Galleria. Of course, I'd been smart and put money away in Mutual Funds. The financial advisor was awesome, but out of all of us, I think I was the only one truly taking his advice. Janine was too concerned with keeping Tony away from her money that she was making stupid decisions and Terrance was on a spending spree that would have him broke in a year. I hoped that they'd come to their senses soon. At least Raquelle wasn't going crazy. She'd barely spent anything, but I guess that's because all that mattered to her right now was her son and her case.

Don't get me wrong, I'd allotted myself a generous spending budget, and I was ready to put it to use.

I reflected on the past two months as I drove down 610. None of us were still working at Clearcast. Terrance went back the Tuesday after we got our money, but I think he only did it so he could make some kind of grand exit. He told me he'd told Evelyn that his rich uncle had died and left him some money so he was out. Then, because he was so loud, the security guard had come in and Terrance had cussed him out on his way out the door.

I lasted one day after that. When Dr. Taylor said he could move my surgery up a week, I turned in my two-hour notice and left.

Of course, folks started putting two and two together and since they knew that we did the lotto pool, and that gossiping Lorna had told folks about the tickets on my desk, they assumed that we had won. My phone had been blowing up. When Owen called me going off, I changed my number altogether.

When I got to the Galleria, I made a beeline to the Gucci store. I definitely was going to buy some clothes, but expensive handbags were my guilty pleasure. I was never a materialistic person but I loved some purses. Even when I didn't have a lot of money, I made sure my budget allotted for me to splurge on a designer bag every six months. Walking into that store and picking out any bag I wanted let me know that I had arrived. I chose the red Soho shoulder bag.

"Nice choice," a deep voice behind me said as I walked away from the counter.

I turned around, and to my surprise, Antonio Whittingham, the star point guard for the Houston Rockets was gazing at me.

"Oh, um, yes, I had been eyeing this style for a while," I said with a smile.

I peered down at the shopping bag I held in my hand, unable to make direct eye contact with him as we stood at the front of the store.

"I love a woman who can walk into a Gucci store and buy what she wants without hesitation," he said.

"And I love being able to buy what I want without hesitation," I replied with a flirty grin.

He stared at me for a few seconds and I felt like he was undressing me with his eyes.

His stellar smile should have been patented and the more I looked at him, the more I felt that he could sense my uneasiness.

"Hi. I'm Antonio." He extended his hand.

Did he honestly think he needed to introduce himself? I had serious doubts that there was one person in Houston, or any other city, that did not know his name. I was weak just looking at him, but I mustered up the strength to give him a handshake. "Nice to meet you, Antonio, I'm Angelique."

He licked his smooth lips. "You are absolutely beautiful, Angelique." The way my name rolled off his tongue gave me goose bumps.

He inched a little closer toward me and I had to shake myself from being intoxicated by his cologne. I was sure that the delayed response made me look like an idiot. I clutched the handles of my purse a little tighter. My new body was feeling things I hadn't felt in. . . ever.

"Thank you." I cleared my throat because I was sure that husky reply was so not cute.

I watched him as casually reached over, picked a pair of aviator style sunglasses and slid them on. He continued to speak as he peered into the rectangular shaped mirror next to the display.

"What do you think about these? Yes or no?"

"Yesss. . . Definitely yessss."

He stood and smiled and I wanted to die.

"I like the way you say that." He motioned for the clerk who came running over.

"Yes, Mr. Whittingham?"

"I need two of these and that belt I was looking at earlier in black and brown."

"Yes, sir, we'll put them on your account," she said, scurrying off.

Gucci had accounts? Now that I was a millionaire, I needed to figure out how to get one.

"Why don't you give me your number so I can take you out. Maybe we can grab some dinner one day this week."

I really wished someone could have pinched me, because I just knew I had to be dreaming. There was no way I was about to get Antonio Whittingham's number in real life. No way. Before my surgery, a man like Antonio wouldn't even give me the time of day.

Even still, I didn't want to appear desperate, even though I wanted to turn cartwheels right there in the middle of the store.

"How about I take your number and call you?" I said, easing my new iPhone 6 out of my purse.

He smiled seductively like he wasn't used to that. But then he rattled off his number as I punched it in.

"I'll call you later," I said like it was no big deal.

He chuckled. "Yeah, beautiful. You do that." He reached out and gave me a hug. "Until then, it was nice to meet you, Angelique."

I didn't want to stop our embrace, but I didn't want to seem too eager so I backed away. "Likewise." I began heading toward the door. I let my small smile morph into a gigantic grin as I rounded the corner to exit the store.

My day had just gone from good to great in a matter of seconds. I couldn't wait to tell Janine and Raquelle about Antonio. People could say what they wanted, but skinny girls got more men. There had been times that I caught men looking at me before the weight loss, but when I would return the glance, they would look away.

The most they would do was smile. Maybe they thought like my mother, *I was pretty to be a big girl.*

That day, I felt good because I knew that the weight I had lost was only the beginning. I strolled down the mall with a grin so huge, and I was sure people thought I was drunk or high. . . maybe both. What they thought of me didn't matter, because for a change, I felt good about myself. One of the hottest, most popular men in the city had just given me his number. Just the thought of calling him made me tingle all over.

And then, I remembered. . . I had a man. Marcus would be heartbroken if he found out what I'd done. I felt momentarily guilty, then I passed by Foot Locker and saw a six-foot-eight cutout of Antonio in his Rockets uniform, advertising the new Adidas. I grinned, pushed aside thoughts of Marcus and tried to decide just how long I would wait to call Antonio.

Chapter 15

Terrance

I was living it up! Yeah, I felt a little bad about the fact that Sheray had basically cut me out of her life. She'd moved out, even refusing any of my winnings. Of course, I thought that was ridiculous, but she'd torn up the check that I'd given her, threw the pieces in my face and told me, "I hope you and your money are very happy." I figured she would come around eventually. But so far, not only had she not come around, but she'd completely cut me off. She'd even changed her cell phone number and told the switchboard at work not to put my calls through. I was a little taken aback at how she was trippin'. But it wasn't anything a night out on the town couldn't fix. And I'd had plenty of nights out.

It was amazing how money could change the caliber of women that you interacted with. I didn't know if word had spread that I hit the lotto or what. I'd told my boy, Mike, but I'd sworn him to secrecy. Even though he claimed he hadn't told anyone, I was starting to think he had because I was suddenly becoming Mr. Popular. I never had been one to hang with a whole bunch of dudes, but Mike and I had turned into party animals. I'd flown him and two of his cousins with me to Vegas two weeks ago, where we'd partied for seven days straight. I finally decided to wrap things up when I realized my bill had reached forty grand.

When I got home, I'd resumed my nightly dating. I wasn't looking for anything serious (Been there, done that). I was just out to have a good time. But the dating scene wasn't all that it had been cut out to be. I told women that I had a rich uncle die and leave me some money because many of them were bold and straight up asked how I "could afford such nice things."

I'd gone out with a woman and not ten minutes into the conversation, she was asking me to pay her light bill. Another woman asked for bail money for her brother. In the beginning, I was loving the ability to just freely give and spend money. But then, it started feeling like someone had put my name and number up on a bathroom wall because I started getting calls left and right. I'd even gone out with Veronica, my old classmate. But she started talking about how she wanted to settle down so I had to drop her.

So these past few weeks, I'd steered clear of the ladies and just partied. Tonight, it was a VIP party for

Houston rapper, Prince Mac. I loved the fact that my newfound wealth allowed me to roll up in my silver Porsche with a booming system. Of course, all eyes were on me as I drove up, got out and tossed the keys to the valet.

Three glasses of Remy Martin VSOP and an appetizer later, I found myself sitting in the VIP section, immersed in conversation with Mia, a woman who was so gorgeous she could have easily been on the cover of any magazine. Her hazel eyes were more intoxicating than the alcohol I'd consumed. I couldn't tell if her long chestnut brown hair was real or not, but it was so well maintained, it didn't matter.

"I haven't enjoyed a conversation like this in a long time," Mia said as she took another sip of her lemon drop martini. She crossed her long, elegant legs and my testosterone kicked up about six notches.

"Neither have I." I paused for a moment, and then I glanced at my watch. It was five minutes after midnight. I was horny and from the looks of it, my wife had no intentions on coming back to me, so I was fair game. Mia was the type of chick you wanted to have on your arm. "You have any plans once you leave here?" I asked. Yeah, I wanted to bed her, but she was the type of chick I wanted around for a while – but just to play with. I definitely didn't want anything serious.

Mia grinned. "I don't, but if you'd like to change that, I just might let you." She raised her eyebrows and finished the rest of her drink.

I don't know if it was the alcohol or what, but I felt compelled to say, "To be sure that we're clear on everything, I want to let you know that I'm not looking for anything serious."

She looked me in the eyes and said, "Serious? What makes you think that I'm not just out to have a good time, too?" Then, she rubbed my forearm. "I can show you a good time, if that's what you're looking for, Big Daddy. No strings attached."

I wasn't expecting her to be so receptive. Knowing that she wasn't expecting anything other than a night of hot sex made me feel much more at ease. "Well, in that case, meet me at Hotel Derek on Westheimer."

The devilish smile on her face let me know that she was down for whatever I wanted to dish. "I'll meet you in the lobby." She licked her lips and eased off the barstool.

As I waited for the bartender to take care of my tab, I watched Mia sashay out of the door. The sexy strut had every man she passed glancing down at her voluptuous behind. She tugged at the short hem on the black spandex dress she wore. And, I could tell she was experienced in walking in stilettos because with every step, she looked more and more like a runway model. My chest was stuck out a bit because I knew within the next hour, I would be the one all up in that.

Once I arrived at the hotel, the valet took my car and I went inside. Mia was seated and when she spotted me, she jumped up and walked with me to the front desk. We checked in and once we got on the elevator, she stood in front of me and kissed me. It was a soft sensual kiss that made me wish the elevator doors hadn't opened, forcing us to stop.

When we got into the room, we wasted no time tearing off our clothes. I was feeling good in all of the right places.

"Hold on, baby," I moaned, reaching into my pocket for a condom. I always kept two in my wallet just in case.

Mia snatched the packet out of my hand, ripped it open, pushed me against the wall, then proceeded to slide it on me. I closed my eyes and moaned in ecstasy.

She stopped, slid on the bed, then used her middle finger to beckon me. I obliged. We kissed and our breathing got heavier as the urge to have our bodies intertwine increased. Her body trembled with anticipation as I entered her and neither of us stopped until we were both satisfied. We rested and then repeated our love dance two more times.

The alcohol must have had more of an influence on me than I realized. I didn't remember falling asleep. But when I woke up, I noticed a slither of light coming in through the dark window dressing. I rubbed my eyes and reached over to touch Mia. My thoughts were that we could have one more ride to ecstasy before it was time to check out. I rolled over, but I felt nothing so I figured Mia had gone into the restroom. "Mia, get your fine self in here, girl."

Nothing.

"Mia?" I furrowed my brows and sat up, only to find that the pile of clothes we'd thrown off of each other were gone. Not one article of clothing was in sight. My eyes darted around the room. My heart pulsed as I kicked the covers off of my legs and jumped out of the bed. I ran into the restroom. No one was in there. I glanced at the nightstand where I'd set my new Rolex. It was gone. "Dammit," I muttered, hitting the corner of the wall with my hand.

As I walked my bare body into the room, I noticed that the only thing Mia left was my valet ticket.

It hadn't dawned on me until moments later that she not only had my clothes, but my wallet. I had over five hundred dollars cash in there, along with my driver's license and credit cards.

I rushed over to the closet and yanked the hotel robe off of the hanger and slipped it on. I loosened my jaws because I noticed I'd started grinding my teeth, which was something I typically did when I was angry. And I was beyond angry. As I thought back to how Mia had snuck into the VIP area, grilled me about whether I was in the music industry, then commented on my Rolex, diamond chain, and Timberlands, I went to the highest level of pissivity. How in the world had I let myself fall for what was clearly a setup?

Walking through the lobby, I understood how it felt to be center stage in front of a large crowd. I couldn't blame the other hotel guests and workers as they stared at a six-foot-three, two hundred and thirty five pound man walking through the lobby barefoot with a robe on.

When I gave the valet the ticket so he could retrieve my car, I was almost sure he laughed at my appearance as he walked away. I was so pissed off that I just ignored him.

When he returned with my car, he got out and looked at me like he was waiting for a tip. I just glared at him as I jumped in the driver's seat and closed the door so swiftly that he had to jump back to avoid getting hurt. I sped off, my mind reflecting back over all the trifling women I'd dealt with these past few weeks. Most of them had been beautiful. Many of them had been their own special kind of crazy. And none of them could hold a candle to my wife.

As I raced toward home, I heard Sheray's voice in my head, "Be careful what you wish for."

Chapter 16

Janine

My cousin was missing in action, and I was trying not to think the worst. It had been three days since I last spoke to him and he wasn't answering my calls or texts.

Every Friday afternoon since he'd claimed the lottery money for me, Darnell and I met at Bank of America. Everybody from the financial advisor to the bank manager, had told us not to put all our money in one bank account. But I couldn't do the mutual fund and investment thing until my divorce was finalized. The advisor had even suggested an offshore account, but I wasn't about to send my money to some strange country. It was just too much to be having Darnell go through all of that anyway, especially when he was using a fake social security number himself. It was just easier to keep it in the bank, and withdraw a little at a time. Once Tony was out of the picture, I would invest and do all that other stuff the financial advisor was suggesting. For now, though, we just would do our weekly withdrawal thing. Now, what I was nervous about was the fact that my name wasn't on the account. I opted not to have my name attached to it because I didn't want Tony to have the slightest chance of getting my money. Our financial advisor told me 'off the record' so he didn't get in trouble, that when Tony filed for divorce I would be bound by law to reveal all bank accounts with my name on them. That was the only reason why I didn't put my name on Darnell's account.

My gut had said that wasn't smart, but my desire to keep Tony away from the money won out. I found out he'd moved in with the Pop-Tart, so I'd be damned if they set up shop on my money.

Even though I hadn't talked to Darnell, I headed to Bank of America. I drove up at five-thirty that afternoon and waited for him until six-fifteen. The lobby closed at six, so I was screwed. After he didn't show up, I called and left a voice message. Darnell knew the routine. I sent text messages and I even called his girlfriend, LaQuanta. She said she had been trying to get in touch with him, too.

I felt my palms getting sweaty. Darnell wouldn't have left me hanging, at least not without calling, and I couldn't think of a time when LaQaunta didn't know where he was.

After another hour passed, I picked up my cell phone and dialed the number to the furniture store where he worked.

"Good evening, thanks for calling Your Furniture Store, this is Barbara. How may I help you?"

"Hi, Barbara. I'm looking for someone who is employed there. I hope you can help me." I was desperate and I didn't have time to waste because for all I knew, my cousin could have been in a horrible car accident or he could have gotten attacked. It wasn't a good thing that my mind always wandered to the worst possible scenario, but I'd been like that all of my life.

"Sure, I can. And if I can't, I can get ya to somebody who can." I heard her eagerness to help through the phone.

"Great, I'm looking for my cousin, Darnell Helms. Can you tell me if he's at work? Or if he came in today?"

"Oh, Honey, Darnell doesn't work here anymore. He resigned last week. He said he -"

I hung up so she wouldn't hear my gasp. My heart was beating so loud I could hear it. "That mother. . ." No, I stopped myself. Darnell wouldn't do this.

I tossed the phone on the seat, and sped out of the Bank of America parking lot and headed to Darnell's duplex. I was going to break in his house if I had to. I needed to find some clue as to where my cousin was.

"Be calm," I told myself on the twenty-minute drive. *Darnell is like a brother to you. You're overreacting.* Even as I had the conversation with myself, I didn't have a good feeling.

I used the radio controls on my steering wheel and blasted the music, hoping to drown out my thoughts.

I barely put my car in park before I jumped out my car and rang his doorbell. After ringing it several more times. I turned to walk back to my car and a taupe Mercedes S550 eased into the driveway. The dark tinted windows prevented me from seeing into the car. But, it didn't take a genius to figure out who it was.

I walked toward the car and Darnell bounced out looking like he'd just robbed a mannequin in Suit Mart. He hit the button on his key ring to lock the doors.

"What's up, cuz?" He flashed all of his teeth, including a brand new gold cap on the side tooth, complete with a dollar sign.

I folded my arms, shifted all of my weight to my left hip, and lifted one eyebrow. "What's up, cuz? That's all you have to say? Have you not been getting any of my phone calls or text messages?"

He didn't look the least bit fazed as he said, "Oh, yeah, I'm gonna have to give you my new number 'cause I'm getting that other one turned off. I got another phone and that old one is somewhere in the house."

I didn't even get into why he had a new phone. Probably LaQuanta. The two of them had a crazy dysfunctional relationship and he'd cut all ties with her one minute, then be back with her the next.

"What's going on? Where have you been? Why didn't you meet me at the bank?"

He paused like he was thinking. "Oh, snap, it is Friday. Girl, since a brother ain't on a time clock, I lost track of the days."

I took a deep breath, grateful that I did indeed know my cousin and he hadn't stolen my money. "Speaking of which, why did you quit your job?"

"Aw, man, I had to bounce on them fools," Darnell said. "They started trippin' cause I came in late a few times. I told 'em straight up that I didn't have to put up with that petty stuff they tried to run at me. So, last week, I was about to clock out for lunch and my manager started talking about I'd better be back on time, so I told her I was out. Shoot, I don't have to take that mess anymore." He shook his head and laughed. "You should've seen her face."

Darnell mimicked the woman's expression like I was really supposed to laugh.

I scratched my eyebrow and rubbed my forehead a few times. "Are you kidding me right now?" I finally said.

He cocked his head to the side and shook it slowly. "I wish I was, cuz. It was epic."

I couldn't believe he was talking as if he found nothing wrong with the situation.

"You are getting out of control," I said.

"What you talking about?" he replied.

"Standing me up."

"Oh, you know I got you." He waved me off like I was making a big deal for nothing.

I sighed. Maybe Darnell was right. The money was making me crazy because I knew my cousin. He had my back no matter what. "Fine. But you could've at least called."

"You right. Sorry about that." He flashed a wide grin.

"And what is that in your mouth?"

"You like?" He turned to the side. "This is my new look. I didn't get it in the front because that's ghetto."

I rolled my eyes. "And what's this?" I said, pointing to the car.

He rubbed his chin hairs and said, "This baby is nice, huh? Fresh off the lot."

"I guess the better question is how did you get approved for a car?"

He smiled. "Shoot, money talks, bullsh-"

"Darnell," I said, getting tired of him, "I know you did not spend my money on a Benz. Take it back and get my money," I demanded.

He held up his hands and smirked. "Hold up. You need to back up off me. You got a car!"

"A used Beamer," I replied.

"Well, I'm not takin' nothin' back. The night you called me, you told me that you were gonna break me off some change. You never mentioned how much or when, so I got it myself."

I took my index finger and poked him in the chest. "Let me tell you something. . . if you don't give me my money, I'll-"

Darnell laughed. "You'll what? Sue me and give the money to Tony and his gal?" He looked at me waiting for a reply I didn't have.

"Cuz, you trippin'," he finally said. "I'm fam. I got you. You know I'm not gonna mess over you." He pulled a wad of money out of his pocket. "I went to the bank earlier." He handed me a large roll. "This is ten grand. And here, I got you some Rush Cards."

"Really?" I said, looking at the prepaid Visa cards from Russell Simmons.

"What? You said you wanted to get the money a little at a time, so Tony wouldn't get suspicious that's what we're doing. I put the maximum of $25-hundred on each card. There are ten of them there, so you ought to be straight for a minute."

I paused, then stuffed the money and cards in my purse. I had taken the first ten grand and paid off bills. I had fifty grand under a mattress. Darnell was right. It's not like I could put the money in the bank just yet.

"How much have you spent?" I asked him.

"Would you just chill?"

"How much, Darnell?"

He sighed like I was really bothering him. "I bought this ride, some gear, a few gifts for folks, but I ain't spent no more than three or four hundred . . . thousand.

I swear I almost toppled over. As much as I hated to admit it, there was nothing I could do about the amount of money he'd already spent or how much he would spend in the future. I couldn't even control how much money he let me withdraw.

As furious as I was, I decided that it was in my best interest to stay on good terms with Darnell because if I didn't, Tony wouldn't be the only one missing out on this fortune. So would I. But I decided at that very moment, family or not, I needed to come up with a Plan B because Darnell was getting a taste of the good life and something was telling me he wouldn't want to give it up.

Chapter 17

Angelique

The pounds were melting off of me like hot wax on a candle. I couldn't pass by a mirror without doing a double take.

My body was banging and my budding relationship with Antonio was giving me a newfound confidence.

I still wasn't completely comfortable naked, but I'd been sucked and tucked so much that my body was dang near perfect – in expensive lingerie. Antonio had no complaints. In fact, we'd spent every other day together for the past two weeks.

"What time do you think you and your mom will be back from seeing your aunt tomorrow?" Marcus spoke louder as I walked from the bedroom into the bathroom to finish packing my duffle bag.

"Probably pretty late so don't wait up for me." I chunked my toiletries in the bag and hoped he wouldn't ask any more questions. I wasn't very good at lying, and in this situation, that was the only choice I had.

At first, it was easy to tell Marcus I would be gone for a few hours or I would leave for an hour or two without any explanation. But lately, Marcus began asking questions. Our relationship had grown stale in the two weeks since I had a taste of being with another man. The only problem was that Marcus didn't seem to think anything was wrong.

Since we'd met, Antonio spoiled me with gifts from designers Marcus probably couldn't even spell. I hadn't told him I won the lottery, but I made it clear that I could buy my own stuff. Still, Antonio wasn't hearing it.

Marcus was a gentleman and I appreciated the way he put my needs before his own. But sometimes, being nice alone just didn't cut it.

Antonio and I had conversations that intrigued me. He also put no pressure on me to leave Marcus because he wasn't looking for a relationship. Other women called him and I knew it. What good would it be for me to care if he talked to other women? He was a huge basketball star, and most women, married or not, would have loved to be in his company.

Antonio made it clear that he was single and loving it. And I loved it, too. I was dabbling in two worlds. Faithful, reliable Marcus at home and sexy spontaneous Antonio on the side.

The Rockets were playing the newly named New Orleans Pelicans and Antonio invited me to the game and told me I could bring a guest. I invited Raquelle. She had been going through a lot emotionally since her son, Shaun was diagnosed with Stage V kidney failure. At first, she was reluctant to accept the invitation because Shaun was scheduled for surgery next week, but her mom insisted that she join me. We all knew she needed to get out of the house and enjoy herself, especially with a looming court case.

"Babe, you're really looking good. Even though I loved you just the way you were, I'm happy that you're happy." Marcus walked up behind me and started caressing my back. When he reached in to kiss the nape of my neck, I hunched my shoulders and wiggled away.

"Not now, Marcus, I'm gonna be late picking up my mom. The ride to Austin is going to take us a while. So I have no time to play."

Lately, I'd been avoiding Marcus and his sexual advances. I really didn't want to have sex with two guys around the same time and since Antonio had been hitting it dang near every day, it left little room for Marcus.

Besides, sex with Antonio made me feel ways Marcus could only dream about. After one dose of that man, Marcus seemed lackluster in his lovemaking skills and was no longer sexually appealing to me.

He reached toward me. "C'mon, Babe. It's been over two weeks since you touched me and now you're about to leave for the night. I mean it was thoughtful of you to offer to drive your mom to see your sick aunt, but before you go take care of her, can you take care of me?"

I felt sorry for Marcus, but not enough to give in. I totally planned to be swinging from the hotel light fixture tonight with Antonio and I didn't want to be nasty and be with two men in one day.

I zipped my bag and put the strap over my shoulder. Then, I reached up and gave him a kiss on his lips. "Sorry, not today." I gave him two quick pats on his chest and walked into the bedroom.

"Well, when? You keep putting me off. We've never gone this long without having sex unless one of us was sick."

I heard Marcus' frustration, but I had to get going. My flight left in a little under two hours and I had to pick Raquelle up from her house. "Stop being such a baby. It's not all about sex. I have a sick aunt that I need to tend to and all you can think about are your selfish, manly needs?"

Instead of replying, Marcus snatched up my bag and said, "I'll take this out to the car for you." No matter how angry Marcus got, I had never seen him lose his temper. I never opened doors for myself, never took out the trash, or never pumped gas if he was around. By far, Marcus was one of the most chivalrous men I knew. And truth be told, he was also very handsome and kept himself up. His broad shoulders and thin waist were always a turn on to me. Pre-Antonio anyway.

As he walked out of the room, I walked over to the full-length mirror I had bought the week before. I glanced at my full figure and couldn't stop the smile that spread across my face. I'd dropped six dress sizes and could see the curves in my hips. I was proud that I could finally tuck in my shirts without feeling self-conscious. No longer did I look in the mirror and see someone who was "pretty for a big girl." I picked up my purse, and walked outside.

As I approached the driveway, Marcus began walking the opposite way toward the house.

"I'll see you some time tomorrow." He didn't respond, so I turned around. "Marcus, did you hear me?"

He didn't turn toward me. "Yep." He opened the door and went inside.

Marcus had never been so short with me. My first thought was to turn around and follow him inside. But I needed to hurry before I missed my flight.

I backed out of the driveway feeling like scum. Was my fling with Antonio worth me possibly losing a man who truly loved me? That was a question I wasn't ready to answer, but I knew sooner or later Marcus would no longer accept me distancing myself from him. No matter how nice he was, I knew that at some point he was going to have enough of my cold-hearted ways.

I couldn't let my mind get consumed with Marcus though because then I'd continue to feel bad and ruin a great time. I decided to do like one of my favorite 90s song said and "Lay back, kick it and enjoy the ride." I'd worry about everything else later.

Chapter 18

Raquelle

Angelique and I had two separate hotel rooms, which didn't really make sense to me on a girl's trip. But she'd said we were millionaires and millionaires didn't share rooms.

I didn't know if it was the money or the weight loss, but Angelique was turning into someone I didn't know. Like the trip here, she'd worn a catsuit. Who the heck still wore catsuits?

When we arrived at the hotel, we decided that we both needed to freshen up before we went to hang out. Angelique said Antonio told her that he wouldn't be able to meet up to go out with us unless they were dismissed from their meetings early, so we planned to have a night out on the town.

I felt guilty for leaving my children at home with my mom, especially Shaun. It was easier for her to stay at my house because Shaun needed to do his dialysis treatments at night while he slept.

No sooner than I'd placed my luggage down in the hotel room, I dialed my mom's cell phone number.

"What do you need, Honey? We're fine," she answered.

"No hello?" I chuckled.

My mom laughed. "Nope. I knew you'd be calling. When the phone rang I told Shaun it was you before I even picked it up."

"What are you all doing?"

"Tiana is on that phone probably taking more pictures of herself to put on the Internet. And, Shaun and I are playing cards."

"Ma, please make sure he doesn't drink too much, and he won't tell you when he gets sleepy, he'll just try to stay up. Don't let him. He needs to get in his bed and do his dialysis treatment. Don't forget he has to do it for eight hours so he'll need to go to bed early enough."

I couldn't think of anything else I needed to remind her of. I just hadn't been away from Shaun in the evenings at any time during the one-month time period that he'd began doing his dialysis at home. Even though I knew my mom would take excellent care of my children, no one could care for them like me.

"Raquelle, honey go ahead and enjoy yourself. We will be fine. I promise Shaun will be in one piece when you return."

I sighed and took a sip of the bottled water I'd been holding in my hand. "Okay, I'll try to call you guys later. We are going to go out and grab a bite to eat."

"It's already after seven. Go eat, hang out, and enjoy yourself. We will just talk to you in the morning before we go to church."

I took a deep breath, realizing how grateful I was to have a supportive mom. "You're right. It will be late when we get back. I'll go ahead and talk to them both now."

I spoke to Shaun and my mom pried Tiana away from her phone long enough for me to tell her goodnight as well.

Once we hung up, I touched up my eyeliner and coated my eyes with a few coats of mascara. Then I picked up my purse, walked across the hall, and tapped on Angelique's door. She swung it open and held up her index finger signaling me to be quiet.

She was on her cell phone. "Yeah, we just got here. And I wanted to call and let you know." She was quiet. Then she said, "She's not doing too well. My mom just went in the back with her. Let me go ahead and get in there with them. I'll give you a call later. Love you, too."

She hung up and tossed her phone on the bed. "That was Marcus. I had to get that over with before we went out and had fun."

I shook my head. "You know I don't like what you're doing to him, right?"

"Yes, you let me know that from the moment I told you about Antonio. But, just wait until you meet him in person. You are going to see why it's hard for me to go back to Marcus."

Angelique had surprised me when she told me she had a male friend on the side. When she told me *who* it was, I was quick to explain that it wasn't a good idea to get involved with athletes, actors, and other famous people unless they specifically tell you they are ready to settle down. They led such busy lives and came in contact with so many people that they rarely settled. She responded by letting me know that she was aware that he did his own thing and that she was just trying to have a little fun.

"And this has nothing to do with the fact that Antonio is a superstar athlete?" I squinted my eyes and tilted my head.

She shook her head. "Of course not. We just have a good time together. He is a really good guy and I enjoy being around him."

"And poor Marcus is sitting at home thinking that you are with your mom?" I had initially rejected her invitation to come to the game because I didn't condone what she was doing as far as Marcus was concerned. He was one of the nicest guys I'd ever met and his love for Angelique was apparent. Most women would beg for a chance to have a man love and treat them like he treated her.

She held up a hanger with a pair of black leggings and a sheer shirt on it. "Okay, Miss Marcus Fan Club president, I know what I'm doing. Give me a minute to get dressed."

I glanced down at my outfit. I had on some skinny jeans with a white tank and some wedge heel sandals. "I'm going to keep this on. I didn't bring a lot of extra clothes."

"And to answer your question, yeah, Marcus thinks I'm with my mom," she called out as she headed into the bathroom. She was quiet for a moment, and then she continued. "I felt bad leaving him at first, but he sounds like he's not even bothered about it."

"You think Marcus is starting to suspect that you are not into the relationship anymore?"

Angelique came around the corner and fixed her clothes as she spoke to me. "No, he's so oblivious to everything. And it's not that I'm not into Marcus. He's a good guy." She did a slow wiggle. "But Antonio? He's great. And can we stop talking about my situation at home? I invited you here so we could have a good time and that's exactly what we are going to do."

She looked at herself in the mirror, first in the front, then she turned for a side view, and finally glanced over her shoulder to look at herself from the back. "You ready?" she said before she leaned over the sink and applied her lipstick.

She was dressed in some black leggings with a sheer red shirt with a leopard bra peeping through. Her black five-inch open toe heels set the outfit off. I knew she was proud of the way she looked and she deserved to feel that way, because she looked amazing. Honestly, anything was better than that hideous catsuit that she wore on the plane.

I surveyed my outfit again. "Yeah, well, I thought I was at first, but now I feel underdressed compared to you." Then, I realized I was here to relax, not catch, since a man was the last thing on my mind. So I was fine as is. "Oh well, I'm not trying to impress anyone so I guess I'm good."

I walked over to Angelique and gave her a hug. "Thanks for inviting me. I didn't realize how much I needed a break."

She smiled at me. And the loving, caring Angelique resurfaced. "Yes, you did. It's written all over your face. I know Shaun will be okay. You are a great mother and I know you're doing all that you can to make sure he gets well soon."

"Aw thanks, I appreciate that."

"It's the truth." She hesitated, then said, "I hate to bring this up, but what's going on with your case at Clearcast?"

I took a deep breath. "Well, I have a court date, but I'm not giving up on settling before court. I'm going by Mr. Perry's office this week, after I get Shaun settled from his surgery and try to work something out."

"Yeah, he's a billionaire, but people with money always want more, so offer him up a few hundred thousand dollars."

I nodded. "That's exactly what I'm going to do. I'm gonna keep my fingers crossed. I don't care how much money I'll have to come up off of at this point. My kids need me. I'd go crazy if I had to be put in jail and some one had to have custody of my kids. And. . . " I felt emotional and I couldn't hold back my tears. "Shaun needs me. He needs me with him. Tiana acts like she doesn't, but she needs me, too. Angelique, what's going to happen to my babies if I get put away?"

I looked at her as if she had all of the answers I needed.

She gave me another hug, then pulled back, and held my shoulders as she spoke with tears in her eyes. She smiled. "You know what? We are not going to speak you going to jail into the universe. We are not going to put our energy into something that may not even happen. But you know what we are going to do? We are going to go out and have a good time. That's what we are going to do." She handed me a tissue, and continued, "I am really sorry I brought this up. But you know what? We both needed to cry. Now we are ready to hit up Bourbon Street."

I sighed and dabbed my eyes. "Yes, you're right. I didn't come here to sulk and think about everything that's going wrong in my life. I am so blessed to have a friend like you. I am so glad you're in my life."

"And, I'm glad you decided to come hang out with me. I knew if anyone deserved a chance to let loose and have some fun, it was you. Now let's go out and show these New Orleans folks what kind of women Texas has roaming around in its streets."

I brought the tissue up to my eyes, wiped away the last of my tears, and checked the mirror to be sure my eye makeup wasn't ruined. Then, I followed her out of the door.

Chapter 19

Terrance

My grandmother used to say, "Folks always want to drink out of somebody's else's well because they think the water is sweeter." I remember as a child, I had no idea what that meant.

But now, after two months of the bachelor life, complete with all the joys that money could bring, I was starting to miss my old boring life. I'll admit I'd had a blast initially, but this mess was definitely getting played out.

After Mia robbed me, I hadn't gone out again. In fact, I had spent the past two weekends at home, alone, thinking about my wife.

Sheray wouldn't even give me a 'bless you' when I sneezed. I got her being angry, but she was going way overboard. I left her name on the bank account and she hadn't even withdrawn any money (Don't get it twisted, I had the bulk of my the money scattered around in different accounts.)

I swung into Pappadeaux to get some sautéed crab fingers to prepare for my lonely night. I had just placed my order when I looked to my right and saw Sheray sitting at a table with another man. To say I was pissed would be the understatement of the millennium. Was this why she wasn't taking my calls? Because she had already moved on? I usually carried myself with class, but it was about to go down right up in here in Pappadeaux.

I stomped over to her table. "So, is there room for three at this little cozy dinner?" I said, grabbing a chair from the table next to Sheray and this strange dude. I slid the chair up to their table and plopped down. "Or is this an intimate twosome thing?"

"Terrance!" Sheray said, shock all across her face. "Wh-what are you doing here?"

"I came to get me something to eat before I went back to our crib. Alone. Something you obviously ain't trying to do."

The guy had the nerve to smile as he extended his hand. "Hi, I'm Charleston."

"Charleston. What kind of name is that?" I sneered. I didn't care how rude I was being. Here I was, sitting up mourning and missing my wife and she was out on a date.

"Terrance!" Sheray admonished.

"It's cool," Charleston laughed. "I'm used to that response."

His calm demeanor was pissing me off. He needed to be scared, very scared.

"Well, I'm Terrance. Sheray's husband," I told him.

Charleston's eyes bucked. He cocked his head and looked at Sheray. "*Husband?* You didn't tell me you were married," he balked.

Sheray was quiet. And my fury went to a whole other level.

"Are you serious? So you're out here with some other dude and you don't even bother to tell him that you're married?" I yelled. I saw people turning their heads to stare at us, but I didn't care.

She leaned in and softly said, "First of all, you need to lower your voice. Secondly, you wanted out, remember? So you don't need to worry who I'm having dinner with."

I glared at her, but said to him, "You know what? I'm not gonna cause a scene, but Charleston, Imma need you to bounce."

The cheesy grin was replaced with a small smile. "Sheray, would you like me to leave?" he asked.

She folded her arms defiantly. "No, I would not. We're having a nice dinner and I don't need it interrupted by my barbaric soon-to-be-ex husband."

"Ex-husband, huh?" I didn't know why those words tore at my insides.

She blew an exasperated breath. "Terrance, you wanted your bachelor life. You got it. You've been searching how to get an annulment. I'm about to give it to you."

It was my turn for my eyes to buck. "Oh, yeah, I saw it on your laptop. I just never said anything. Then when you got your money, you lost your damn mind and determined you didn't need me. So, I'm letting you go find your mind. In the meantime, you go do you and I'll continue to do me."

Charleston grinned. "And she does her very well."

Oh, this fool was trying to get straight punched in Pappadeaux. I stood and leaned over him. "Man, I will knock th-"

Charleston jumped up, too. "Touch me and I'll sue you for all your lotto winnings."

That made me pause. "So not only is my wife up here with this other dude, but you're telling him my business. Really, Sheray? So this is how things are now?" I asked.

She was unfazed. "This is how you made them, Terrance."

All of my bravado went out the window and I felt a sudden pang in my heart. Sheray was so cold, so unmoved. Did that mean she was really moving on?

"What do you want, Terrance?" she finally said, motioning for Charleston to sit back down.

"I want to talk to you. Alone," I said, cutting my eyes at Charleston.

"I don't have anything to say."

As I stood over that table, I figured I had three options: I could leave, I could act a fool, or I could pour my heart out and fight for my wife. This guy was lame-looking. No way she'd choose him over me.

"Why are you with this guy?" I found myself saying. "This is what you want?" I pointed at him. This dude looked like he had stepped right off one of those runway reality shows. "He's looking all suspect."

Charleston put his hand to his chest and feigned shock. "Well, damn. I need to work on my wardrobe because I don't need anyone *suspecting* anything about me. I need them to know for sure."

I didn't know what he meant by that and I didn't really care.

Sheray glared at me. "He's not suspect."

"You're naive, Sheray," I said.

"He's not suspect because he's straight out gay."

"What?"

"How you doin'?" Charleston said, giving me a Wendy Williams impersonation before bursting out laughing.

"This is my friend," Sheray said. "Pink, from New York."

"Your friend that you grew up with?" I asked, suddenly wishing I had never come to their table.

"Yeah, I don't go by Pink anymore," Charleston said with a grin. "Now, I prefer Pastel or Plum."

"Oh, ah, but he said he didn't know you were married," I stammered. I felt like a bonafide fool. Even the people at the two tables next to us were snickering at the show that I'd just put on.

"He was being funny since you came over here acting like a caveman," Sheray said, a scowl plastered across her face. "Charleston was in town and we decided to have dinner. Nothing more."

I looked apologetically at Charleston, but no words would come out of my mouth.

The expression on my face must have given him joy because he smiled and raised his wine glass. "Apology accepted. I get it, though. I always told Sheray she was going to drive some man crazy."

Was I crazy now? Judging by the way people all around the restaurant were staring at me, that answer would be a resounding yes.

"Terrance, go home," Sheray said. "Go back to your bachelor pad. You're living *La Vida Loca*. And rest assured, as long as I'm still your wife, I won't be seeing any other guys."

Now I was not only embarrassed, I felt guilty as hell.

Chapter 20

Angelique

"All right girl, I'll catch up with you in the morning," I said to Raquelle as I slid my key card in the door.

She yawned as she unlocked her hotel room door. We'd had a blast on Bourbon Street. I was loving all the attention the men were giving me. Never in my life had I had so many men offer to buy me drinks. The only reason I turned them down was because I didn't want to be drunk when I saw Antonio later.

"Good night," Raquelle said, her words slurred because she did take several guys up on their offer. Raquelle had partied like she was on her last days of freedom. I was remaining hopeful, but I was glad to see her let her hair down. "Have fun and don't do anything I wouldn't do tonight."

I put my hand over my mouth and looked up while I batted my lashes. "I have no idea what you're talking about."

Raquelle shook her head. "Mmm hmmm. . . I'll bet you don't. Go on and get freshened up before your company comes."

She stumbled inside her room. I debated going in and making sure she got in bed, but I glanced at my watch. I only had about ten minutes to get prepared for Antonio's arrival. While Raquelle and I were hanging out, Antonio called and told me he was ready to see me. I promptly told Raquelle that we would have to cut our night out short and since she was on the verge of passing out, she was okay with that.

When I got out of the shower, I lathered down in my Carol's Daughter Goddess Soufflé, then slipped on my black lace teddy that I'd purchased online and had sent overnight delivery. It fit me just right, and squeezed in that excess skin around my belly enough to boost my confidence even more. I tucked the left side of my shoulder length hair behind my ear and allowed the right side to hang in my face. Then, I dabbed some golden musk fragrant oil behind each ear and rubbed a little bit on each of my inner thighs just in case Antonio decided to give me some kisses down low. The thought of him burying his head between my thighs made me feel like I had fire in my loins.

No sooner than I'd put on my play list of lovemaking music, which started off with R. Kelly's "Get Up on a Room," I heard three quick knocks on the door. I ran over and turned on the lamp near the bed and I flipped the main light in the room off. I swung the door open.

"Hey," I said as I grabbed him by the neck and started planting kisses on his lips, making sure that I slightly bit and sucked on his bottom lip just the way he liked it. My new body had given me the confidence to bring out my inner freak and I was ready to unleash her on Antonio.

"Mmm. . . Baby, you look so good." He stepped into the room and closed the door. He held my right hand and lifted his arm to toward the ceiling. "Spin around so I can see it from the back. That's my favorite view."

I did as I was told. Whenever I was around Antonio I could never stop smiling like a schoolgirl who got asked out by her longtime crush.

"Thank you for violating your eleven o'clock curfew to come hang out with me," I said.

His bedroom eyes were locked on me and he spoke huskily. "I wouldn't do it if I didn't feel like it was worth it. And looking at how fine you are, it's definitely worth it." He unbuckled his pants and took them off along with the rest of his clothes. "I don't have much time." He sat on the edge of the bed. "Now, come here and give me what I need."

I walked over to him and rubbed his chiseled chest as I ran my tongue over his stomach. His breathing intensified as I continued kissing him. He nudged my head to continue traveling down with my kisses. I followed his lead. He panted and moaned and right before he climaxed, he moved me off of him and slipped on a condom. I straddled him and didn't stop until we were both satisfied.

I climbed off of him in pure bliss. "As usual, that was great." I couldn't picture a better way to end my night.

"Yep, no doubt." He slapped my behind, then sat up and grabbed his underwear and his jeans.

I flipped over on my side, wrapped myself in the sheets, and rested my head in my hand. "Do you have to leave so soon?"

"Yeah, I do. I gotta get back to my room before they notice I'm gone." He stepped into his clothes.

"Aw, too bad. I wish we could lie in bed and cuddle. We've never done that before." Each time we'd been intimate he had something to do immediately afterward.

"Naw, Sweetheart, I don't do the whole cuddling thing. That leads to expectations and extra attachments that I ain't lookin for." He slid his shirt on.

I squinted. "Oh. I see. So you just came up here to my room to hop in bed, get pleasured, and then burn off?" I would have been lying to myself if I said I didn't care that Antonio didn't seem to be feeling me as much as I was feeling him. My mixed emotions were confusing me. If I had no intention of leaving Marcus, why was I suddenly wondering what life would be like as Antonio's girl?

He stood and faced me as he straightened his shirt. "I told you, I'm all about a good time. Right now, I don't have time to be tied up in a relationship. I'm concentrating on my career and I have too much going on to have to answer to anyone."

I sat up and fumbled for my clothes. The conversation made me feel awkward being naked. "I just thought, I mean, we haven't been hanging out long but I was just wondering if I was the type of girl -"

"The type of girl that what? Can make me settle down? See that's what I don't get about you broads. You think as soon as you hop in bed with a man that he's yours. Tell me now, either you're down with being cool with me or we can end this now."

He glared at me as he waited for a response. I didn't know what to say. It wasn't that I thought Antonio would drop things he had going on in his personal life to be with me, but at the same time, I didn't think I was just an extra way for him to pass time. I just knew that being able to hang out with Antonio and be invited to his game, as his guest was something millions of women wished they could do.

"Okay, you're reading way too much into things," I said, trying to play it off. "I know how this goes, you do you, and I do me."

"Exactly." He leaned in and kissed me. "And we do each other. Very well, I might add." He smiled. Then he took his index finger and put it under my chin and lifted my face so that I looked at him. "So are we good?"

I sat on the bed gazing up at him as I nodded with a forced smile. What the heck was I doing? I had a man yet I was sitting here feigning after someone who made it clear what he wanted.

"All right, let me get back down to my room so I can get some rest," he said.

I stood and walked behind him as he went to the door. "I hope you have a good night," I said as he left out.

"You too. See ya at the game tomorrow."

I shut the door, then leaned up against it. I wasn't going to lie, that entire exchange hurt. But what I couldn't figure out was why. I knew the game so why in the world was I trying to change the rules?

Chapter 21

Janine

It was taking everything in my power to keep my cool. I couldn't believe Darnell. Another Friday, another no-show at the bank. And he still wasn't answering my calls or texts.

He's just caught up, I told myself. No way would my cousin screw me. Even still, I'd decided I was going to withdraw all the money and put it in some no-name little bank and pray that Tony never found out. I just couldn't take the stress with Darnell. That's what he was supposed to be meeting me at the bank to do, and he once again, hadn't shown up.

My doorbell rang and my heart jumped, hoping it was Darnell. That was the only thing that made me swing the door open without looking out the peephole.

"Owen?" I said, looking at my former coworker. He'd been over my house once before because he and my husband were in a basketball league together. But I didn't know that they hung out enough for him to randomly show up on my doorstep. At least that's why I hoped that he was here.

"Hey, what's up?" I said, not moving from the door. My son was asleep and I didn't need him waking up to a strange man in our living room.

Owen leaned against the doorframe. "Just checking in to see how things are going with you."

I'm sure he could see my confusion. "Uh...I'm okay. Just got a lot going on."

"Yeah, well is there something that I can help you with?"

I wasn't even going to try and pretend that I was interested in anything he had to say. "I don't know whether you heard, but Tony doesn't live here anymore."

"I know. I ran into him at the post office yesterday and he told me. Sorry to hear things didn't work out."

If he knew Tony no longer lived here, that meant that he was here for only one reason.

"We miss you at Clearcast," he said.

"Yeah, I had to go," I said, still not moving from the door.

Finally, he said, "Can I come in?"

"It's not a good time."

He pushed past me and walked inside. "Aww, don't be like that."

"Owen, really?" I said, following him back into my living room. "I was just heading out. I don't have -"

"I'm not going to keep you long," he said, turning to face me. "I just want to check on you."

"Well, I'm fine. So now you can go." I pointed toward the open door.

"So, we can't chat?"

I bit my bottom lip and tried to keep my cool. "What do you really want?"

"I told you that I wanted to check on you. Oh, and I wanted to congratulate you."

That made me pause.

"Congratulate me for what?" No one at work was supposed to know that I had won the lottery. Granted, we'd heard rumors that people thought we'd won, but since we opted out of the public press conference, no one knew for sure. And I definitely wasn't about to confirm anything with Owen.

"I want to congratulate you on hitting it big." A cocky smile spread across his face. "I know y'all tried to be low key, but how many conversations did we have about all the great things we were gonna do when we hit that lotto?"

I tried to act like his statement was ludicrous. "What are you talking about?"

"One of the things we both said we were going to do was walk in and tell Evelyn we were quitting, and walk out like a boss. So imagine my surprise when I heard that was exactly what you did. I know Raquelle got fired, but you quit. Angelique and Terrance quit. All the people that used to play the lotto pool are gone. Except me."

"And your point would be?"

"All y'all leaving at the same time. That didn't seem right, it just couldn't have been a coincidence. So I went and looked and a JART Trust claimed the jackpot that week. JART. Janine, Angelique, Raquelle and Terrance." He smiled confidently like he was proud of himself for figuring it out.

"What are you talking about, Owen?" My tone was exasperated as I pointed around my living room. With the exception of the big screen TV I'd recently bought, my surroundings looked pretty meager. "Look around here! Does it look like I won the lotto?"

He glanced around, turning his nose up. "So? For some reason, you haven't spent your money yet."

I sighed. "Why are you here?"

"Because I think it's foul how y'all cut me out."

I wanted to tell him that he was the one that said he didn't want to play that week, but I didn't want to give him any ammunition.

"I always play the lotto with y'all and it's wrong for you guys to cut me out just because I didn't play that week. We should be in this together. You know I deserve a cut of that money." He no longer sounded like he was cocky and playing games. He sounded angry.

"Then you need to go talk to the people from JART Trust because I don't have anything to offer," I calmly replied.

"You guys are JART! Don't play me. And Angelique won't return my calls and you know Terrance doesn't cut for me. So I figured you would be the voice of reason." He slowly began pacing around my living room. "Then, as if God agreed with me, I was in the barbershop last week and my barber, Benny, was bragging about his boy that came into a buttload of cash because he hit the lotto. And then when Benny said his name, Darnell Helms, I kept thinking, where do I know that name from because it's not like there are a lot of Helm's around here? Then it dawned on me, Janine Helms Weathers. That's what it says on your plaque on your desk. Of course my mind started racing. I checked and there was no record of a Darnell Helms winning the lotto. Then, when I bumped into Tony and he told me y'all split and it was pretty ugly, it all started to make sense. You won the lotto, but you had someone related to you claim the money so that your estranged husband didn't get any of your winnings. Stop me when I get to the good part." He grinned like he'd just solved some big puzzle.

I glared at him, but didn't respond. "And the way I see it, that piece of information opened the door for the possibility that I could get my hands on some of that money, too."

I wanted to tell him that I couldn't even find Darnell right now, so his efforts to strong-arm me out of some money were futile.

"I don't know what you want from me, but I'm stressed, I don't have any money," I said instead.

He pointed outside my window. "Then, how'd you get that new BMW?"

I closed my eyes and inhaled. The one thing I'd bought myself had come back to bite me in the butt.

"It's none of your business how I got anything," I said. "And even if your cockamamie theory was true, I don't know what you want from me."

"I want in on the money."

I marched over to the door. "Boy, bye."

He glared at me as he inched toward me. "I wonder if Tony knows about your winnings? I can't imagine he does since he was collecting mail when I saw him. Maybe I should go ask him."

That made my insides turn flips. But I couldn't let Owen know that he was rattling me. "Tell him what you want. And I'll tell him just like I told you, I'm broke."

"Whatever. You're foul, that's what you are," Owen said.

I held the door open. "Bye, Owen."

All his confidence and cockiness was gone as he slowly walked out the door. "This ain't over," he said, stepping outside. "You're making a bad choice. One way or the other you're going to pay. Trust me, my way is a lot cheaper. I only want a mil."

I didn't even reply as I slammed the door in his face. It was bad enough that I had to worry about Darnell, but now, I had to wonder how long it would be before Tony found out because judging from the look on Owen's face, it *was* just a matter of time.

Chapter 22

Angelique

It was just after ten o'clock when I walked into my house.

"Marcus, I'm home," I yelled as I walked through the living room. I'd tried calling him three times since my plane landed and he hadn't returned one call.

I found it unusual that Marcus hadn't met me at the door to grab my bag. As I walked upstairs, I heard the television in our room. I was sure he'd fallen asleep watching a movie and didn't realize when I came in.

When I got to my bedroom, Marcus didn't budge. He was lying in bed on his back with both arms tucked behind his head, watching ESPN Sportscenter.

"Hey, I tried calling you a few times before I got home. Have you been sleep?" I set my bag down and walked toward him as I waited for his response.

"No, I've been wide awake." He never looked away from the television screen. "In fact, I'm more awake than ever." He was staring at the TV so intently that I wondered if he was even watching it.

"Are you okay?" I asked.

"I'm fine."

His response was dry and short. The moments that followed were filled with an awkward silence. "Is everything okay?" I hated when people asked questions they already knew the answers to, but I couldn't help it. I knew Marcus, and I knew everything wasn't okay. It was unlike him to miss a phone call or text message without returning it, and then when I came home, he didn't even acknowledge me.

My question was met with silence.

"Are you feeling all right?" I reached over to feel his forehead with the back of my hand and he slid his head out of my reach.

"I'm fine." He sat up on the edge of the bed. "How's your Aunt Brenda?"

I relaxed. Maybe my guilt was getting the best of me. "Oh, she's doing a little better. She insisted that my mom and I come back home even though she wasn't fully well."

"Hmmm. . . that's interesting." He turned to look me directly in the eye. "Did you drop her off in Austin after you and Raquelle left the basketball game in New Orleans?"

I gulped. *How did he know I was at the basketball game?* There were only a handful of times in my life when I had been at a loss for words and this was one of them.

Marcus shook his head. The pained expression on his face was enough to make me want to cry.

I cleared my throat. "Look, Marcus, I didn't mean to lie to you." I attempted to put my hand on his shoulder.

He jerked away like I had a contagious rash. "Don't touch me, Angelique. You say you didn't *mean* to lie, yet you made up a whole story about your aunt being sick." He shook his head. "And to think, I actually believed your lies. I thought my mind was playing tricks on me when I saw you hollering in the crowd at the basketball game. Then, the camera zoomed in closer and I saw you and Raquelle clear as day."

Pain shot to the back of my throat. Stupid cameras. There had to be three hundred thousand people in that arena. Why in the world would they zoom in on us? I was totally oblivious to the fact that I had been on TV. There should have been some type of clause that prevented film crews from putting people on television without their knowledge.

"Look Marcus, I never meant to hurt you. I guess that's why I made up that story about Aunt Brenda." I couldn't bring myself to look him in the eyes. "I just wanted to get away and have some fun in New Orleans."

"And you had to lie to do it?"

I moved closer to him. It used to be difficult for me to lie to Marcus. I didn't know why it was coming so easy now. "Babe, I'm sorry. I just didn't think that you would approve. Raquelle invited me and well. . . I should've just been honest."

"You don't even know what that word means." Marcus stared at me so hard, he could have pierced a hole in me with the rage in his eyes. "You know the craziest part of all of this is that I told myself that there had to be a valid reason as to why you lied to me," he continued. "But my gut wouldn't let it go, so I logged into your laptop and saw your iMessages. You and Antonio Whittingham's iMessages."

"You read my messages?" I cried, only because I didn't know what else to say.

"Yep," he said, with no shame. "And I saw all the sexy photos in your photo stream. Photos that you never sent to me." He frowned as he stood up. "Guess they weren't taken for me. By the way, you might want to turn off your iCloud."

"I can't believe you went snooping," I said, at the same time not believing that I'd been dumb enough not to turn off my iCloud backup.

He glared at me. "And I can't believe you cheated on me."

"I. . . I, you. . . I can't believe you went in my personal stuff."

"Don't try to turn this around on me," he snapped. "Yeah, I shouldn't have gone snooping because when you look for stuff, you usually find it. I looked and I found." He brushed past me and entered the walk-in closet.

My feet seemed cemented to the floor because I couldn't move. I didn't know if I was more shocked to learn that Marcus found out I was in New Orleans or if my guilt planted me where I was. Whichever was the case, it took me a few moments to move. I closed my eyes and took a few deep breaths.

Marcus returned to the bedroom with a duffle bag. It was then that I noticed that his dresser drawers were empty.

He didn't say another word as he headed into the hallway.

"Where are you going?" I asked, following him.

"Anywhere but here." His feet thudded down the steps and I followed close behind him.

"Don't you think we should talk about this?" I stood in front of the door that led to the garage.

"Move, Angelique." Marcus reached around me and tried to open the door.

"No. I'm sorry. I need to explain."

Then, he did something I didn't expect. He balled up his fist and hit the door over my head, a move that made me flinch in fear. "Angelique, move out of my way before I move you."

Instead of moving out of his way, though, I folded my arms, pressed my back against the door, and firmly said, "I won't move until you tell me when you're coming back." Until that moment, I had never understood why women stood in front of doors to hold their men hostage. But I got it now. I wouldn't let him leave like this. Marcus wasn't giving me answers and although I was the guilty party, I needed to know what he was thinking.

"I'll be back tomorrow." He paused, then added, "to get the rest of my things. Now, will you move out of my way?" When I still didn't move, he said through gritted teeth, "I know you think I'm Mr. Nice Guy, but you really don't want to see me at my worst. Now, move your cheating ass out of my way."

The venom in Marcus' eyes told me now was not the time to try him, so I did as I was asked.

As Marcus walked past me, he turned and said, "I hope you find whatever it is that you're looking for. But, you can do it without me. I'll save you from having to think of more lies to tell. The new you sucks. I'd take big Angelique with the big heart over this skinny, conniving, lying tramp any day."

A sudden coldness hit me at my core. Marcus wasn't supposed to break up with me. I was the one that had gotten bored with him. But I never wanted us to truly break up. I opened my mouth, but no words escaped.

Marcus turned the doorknob and stepped into the garage. He gave me a harsh squint and said, "You might be enjoying the smaller version of yourself, but you were a much better person when there was more of you to love." Then, he closed the door.

If the saying "sticks and stones may break my bones, but words will never hurt me" were true, then why did I feel like I'd just gotten punched in the stomach?

Chapter 23

Raquelle

Money might not be able to buy happiness, but it sure could put you in the vicinity of it. That's all I could think as I looked down at my son. He was trying his best to be strong, but I could tell that all the needles and contraptions hooked up to him had him terrified.

"You okay, big boy?" I asked, squeezing his hand.

He nodded, but didn't say anything.

"You know Mama loves you? I'm gonna be there the whole time." I stroked his hair. Tiana stood next to me. Usually, she was unfazed about everything, but fear was written all over her face.

"He's going to be just fine," I assured her, stroking her long, box braids.

She leaned down and kissed Shaun on the forehead. "Hurry up and pull through because I need to beat you at Madden."

"You don't even play Madden," Shaun replied.

Her voice cracked as she said, "Get better and I will."

He forced a smile, then turned and looked at me. "Is this gonna work, mama? Will I be better after this?"

"That's our prayer, baby." I didn't know what our future held so I had already paid for the surgery in full, as well as paid for at-home medical care for the next three years. My prayer was that I would be there and would only need the nurse to supplement my care. But I paid for full-time care just in case.

"Mama, why did this happen to me?" Shaun asked. He was in the bed, waiting to wheeled out to begin his transplant surgery. "Did I do something bad as a baby?"

"That's not the way God works, Sweetie. He doesn't punish His children." I leaned over and kissed him on the forehead, too. "They have to get you in there and get prepped, then I'll be right in. I love you."

"To the moon and back," he replied as the nurse pulled up the side railing on the bed.

"Give us about fifteen minutes," the nurse said.

I nodded and struggled to fight back tears as they wheeled my baby out.

"He's going to be okay," my mother said, coming up behind me and wrapping her arm around me. I'd forgotten that she was here. But of course, she would be. If my father were alive, he'd be here, too. My family was close knit and if anything ever were to happen to me, the only comfort I would have is knowing my family would take good care of my children.

I welcomed my mother's touch. "He has to be okay." I sighed as I stared at the door they'd just wheeled my son out of. We stood in silence for a few minutes, then I said, "Mama, how do you stay strong, watching your child go through something like this?" My older sister had died of lupus when she was thirteen. I barely remembered it, but I did recall the toll it had taken on my mother. "I'm trying to stay faithful, but I don't understand why my son is going through this."

"Some things aren't for us to understand," my mother replied, removing her arm and turning me to face her. "You just have to stay faithful. That's what faith is, believing when you can't see. But think about it, you've already been blessed. A person is more likely to get struck by lightening than win the lottery. Yet, you won the lottery and that meant that you were able to give your son something that just a few months ago, you had no idea how you'd be able do it, so don't tell me God ain't good. Instead of looking at what you don't have, count your blessings for what you do." She squeezed my chin. "Now, go change so you can be with your son."

"I love you, Mama."

"I love you, too, baby."

I hugged her, then Tiana, then headed into the bathroom to change into the scrubs they told me I had to wear. I couldn't be in the room during the actual surgery, but I could go in with him until the anesthesia knocked him out. I'd just put on the shoe covers when my phone beeped to let me know that I had an incoming text message.

Mr. Perry has agreed to see you. Next Monday. 1 pm. 10 minutes – Elsa

My first instinct was to allow the glimmer of hope to set in. Elsa was Mr. Perry's assistant. I had waited for her after work last week and begged her (okay, offered her ten grand) to convince Mr. Perry to give me ten minutes. I don't know what she'd said to get him to agree to, but I said a silent prayer of thanks, then dropped my phone back in my purse and pushed the purse into one of the dressing room lockers. Today would be all about Shaun. Tomorrow, I would worry about my future.

Chapter 24

Janine

I didn't know why I thought I would get answers from my aunt, Ora. In her eyes, Darnell - her miracle baby when she was 46 years old – was right up there on the rolls with St. Peter. Forget the fact that he was always getting into trouble, petty trouble like fighting, vandalism, drinking and driving, but trouble nonetheless.

According to Aunt Ora, everything Darnell did wrong was because someone was out to get him. But I hoped the fact that I was family would convince her to help me find Darnell.

"Hey, baby," my aunt said, swinging open her screen door and motioning for me to come inside her small wood frame home. I'd decided to go by her house after a sleepless night. I was now convinced Darnell had skipped town with my money. Now, I just needed to find out where he'd gone. "How have you been? I see you've been eating good," she said, patting my hips as I passed.

In my family, you had to have thick skin because they called it like they saw it. I always knew it was done in love, so I was cool with that.

"Just trying to see if you've seen Darnell?" I sat down on her sofa. The crunch of the plastic caused me to shift as I tried to get comfortable.

"Not in a couple of days." Aunt Ora shook her head as she sat down in her tattered recliner. "He was over here last week with that harlot he calls a girlfriend. Chile got three kids and four baby daddies."

I didn't even bother asking my aunt how that was even possible. She was forever spewing some off-the-wall rationales.

"I really need to get in touch with him," I said.

It was then that I noticed a mink stole hanging on the coat rack.

"Wow, Auntie, what's that?"

"Ooooh," she said with a big smile as she jumped up, then walked over and picked it up off the rack. "Isn't it nice?" She wrapped it around her shoulders and stroked it like it was the softest thing that she'd ever touched. "I told Darnell I don't have anywhere to wear this but my baby said I deserve the finer things."

I gritted my teeth. It wasn't that I was against buying Aunt Ora anything, but I couldn't appreciate Darnell buying folks gifts with my money. And a mink stole in Houston was a waste of money, especially for my aunt who wouldn't set foot outside if the temperature dropped below fifty degrees.

"How did Darnell afford a mink stole?" I asked, wondering what lie he'd told his mother. Darnell knew like I did. If he told her about the lotto money, she'd tell everyone dating back six generations.

"My baby got a promotion," Aunt Ora said. "They made him vice president of that furniture company."

If I wasn't so mad, I would've burst out laughing. Darnell didn't even have a GED. How my aunt thought he'd be a vice president was beyond me.

"Do you know where he is, how I can get in touch with him?" I asked.

"He said they were sending him to the Bahamas for training," she proudly replied.

"The Bahamas?"

"Yes, he's so important. You know they send their important folks away for training. He's been there all week." She gently hung the stole back on the coat rack, petting it like it was some kind of animal.

I was seething. Darnell didn't even have the decency to tell me that he was going out of town.

"Did he say when he'd be back?"

"He didn't, but he promised to take me to the eye doctor on the 16th," she replied. "These cataracts shole been bothering me. I was trying to watch 'Deal or No Deal' and that Wayne Brady was a big ol' brown blur."

"Okay, Auntie," I said, cutting her off before she continued running down her list of ailments. "If you talk to him, please tell him that I really need to get in touch with him."

I wanted to tell her the truth, that he'd stolen my money, but number one, I'd have to explain what money. Number two, I wasn't completely sure that Darnell had stolen anything. My cousin would kill for me so I was having a hard time believing he'd steal from me. More likely he was caught up in the lifestyle the money brought. At least I hoped so. And number three, it wasn't like Aunt Ora would believe anything bad about Darnell anyway.

"You still at Clearcast?" she asked. "You want me to see if Darnell can hire you? I told your mama, God rest her soul, that I would watch out for you. And I just think you were destined for something better than sitting up there answering telephone calls. No disrespect to an honest day's work, but you should go for a management position like Darnell."

And on that note, I knew it was time to go.

"All right, Auntie. Just please if you talk to him, let me know."

It took me another ten minutes, of declining food, trying to interrupt her and listening to the latest neighborhood gossip, before I could get out the door.

I had just gotten back in my car when my phone rang. I wasn't in the mood to deal with anyone, but I saw Angelique's name pop up and I hadn't talked to her in almost three weeks.

"Hello."

My greeting was met with tears. It took a few minutes, but I finally calmed Angelique enough to decipher what she was saying.

"What do you mean he's gone?" I asked.

She took a deep breath as if she was trying to pull herself together, then Angelique filled me in on everything about her cheating, Marcus finding out and ultimately leaving her. I felt bad that she'd been going through all of that and I had been so wrapped up in my own drama that I hadn't noticed.

"I'm so sorry, Angelique. I had no idea."

"Can we just talk about something else?" she finally said. "I can't deal with this anymore. What's up with you?"

I debated filling her in on my drama. Angelique had warned me to be careful with my money, but I'd assured her that Darnell wouldn't mess over me. "You might have been right," I said. "I think my cousin has screwed me. I can't find him and he's stopped answering my calls and texts."

"Are you kidding me?" she exclaimed.

Before I could reply, my other line beeped and I glanced down to see Owen's number on my caller ID.

"Owen is calling me," I groaned.

"What does he want?"

"I don't know. You know he came over, all but threatening me if we didn't give him any money."

"You didn't confirm that we won did you?"

I pushed the Decline button and continued talking. "Girl, no. But he's been playing Sherlock Holmes and digging around. He even knows about the trust, but I told him he was crazy."

"Come to think of it, he left me a couple of messages," Angelique said.

"Well, he threatened to tell Tony."

"Do you think he will?"

I shrugged like she could really see me. "I'll cross that bridge when I get to it. Right now, I'm just praying there will be some money left when I finally find my cousin."

Chapter 25
Angelique

It had been four days since Marcus had come to get the rest of his belongings and not one time had he attempted to call me. I didn't know where he was staying and it was driving me crazy to know that the man who'd loved me more than I loved myself had walked out of my life.

I'd called, sent text messages, and I even left a few voice messages apologizing to him. If the roles were reversed, I probably wouldn't have spoken to him either. I could understand his pain. As far as I knew, Marcus had been honest and faithful to me. I'd messed up a good thing.

It wouldn't have been so bad if I hadn't felt so alone. Antonio and I hadn't spoken since we'd left New Orleans. I'd received a missed call from him Monday after Marcus had come back to gather his things. But, when I called him back, I got no answer even though it was only thirty minutes later. I knew if I didn't answer when he called, I'd have to wait until his schedule cleared to talk to him again. The pattern had been the same since the beginning. Of course I had been sending text messages, but he didn't bother responding.

Although it was early, I decided that I would go home and curl up in my bed. Netflix and wine were about to become my new best friends.

Raquelle's son had come home from the hospital yesterday. And thankfully it looked like he was going to be just fine, but I knew nothing would convince her to leave his side. Janine was dealing with her own drama trying to find Darnell. I told her that was crazy for her to be giving anyone that kind of power over her money. Family or not, greed had a way of trumping everything. Since I didn't have anyone to hang out with, I decided to just spend another evening alone. Maybe I'd get lucky and Antonio would call.

I had gone to grab a bite to eat and as I cruised home, Toni Braxton's velvety voice surrounded every inch of my car's interior. As she crooned "Another Sad Love Song," I batted my eyes as fast as I could. I even turned the air conditioner on full blast to help me fight back the tears.

When my phone rang, I glanced at the caller ID and eagerly yanked it off the charger and cleared my throat. "Hello?"

"What's up?" Antonio's voice changed my mood instantly.

"Nothing my way. What's up with you?" For the first time in days, a smile crept on my face.

"Aw, nothing much. Just chillin' at the crib. I was wondering if I left my watch in your hotel room Sunday night."

"No, I didn't see it." I wanted to add that he wouldn't have thought he'd forgotten anything if he hadn't rushed off. It was a disappointment to know that he'd only called to ask about a stupid piece of jewelry after we hadn't spoken in several days. "I thought you might have been calling to let me know how much you missed me." I awaited his response.

He chuckled. "Of course I miss you, Baby. I've just been busy, that's all. I know you understand."

"Yeah, I do. I can't wait to see you again, though." My heart fluttered just thinking about Antonio's tongue working it's magic.

"The feeling is mutual. Trust me. You know how it is when we get together. I'll make it a point to see you before this week is over."

"Sounds great. Maybe I can cook dinner for you one night."

"That sounds like a plan to me. But, hey, let me hit you up later. I'm at home about to get my workout on."

"I wish I was there to see you flexing," I said flirtatiously.

"I wish you were here, too, Babe."

"I could be there in twenty minutes." I didn't want to appear desperate, but I really didn't want to sit around the house and think about all that I'd lost. I wanted to be with Antonio. I wanted to feel like my loss was not in vain.

"Ah, well, you know, if . . . " His words trailed off.

In the short time I'd been with him, I'd never known Antonio to mince words.

"What? If what?"

"You know what?" he said, that usual cockiness returning. "Why don't you come on and roll through? You'd be the icing on my cake tonight."

That brought an even bigger smile to my face. "On my way. Can't wait to feel those lips," I said.

"Yeah. I can't wait either."

I don't know why, but he sounded more excited than ever. Maybe he really missed me, too. Maybe I could salvage something with Antonio so I wouldn't have lost Marcus for nothing.

When I hung up, I turned the radio back up and bounced to the music. It was amazing how that phone call lifted my spirits.

I was almost at home, so I decided to dip in and change. I ran into my house and jumped in the shower. I slipped into the sexiest lingerie I had, then wrapped my knee length pea coat over my body. I would have never had the courage to do anything like that prior to my surgery.

What are you doing? This isn't even you? As I stood staring at myself in the mirror, I couldn't help but ask myself that question. Unlike Terrance, the money hadn't made me lose my mind, but the weight loss had. The weight loss had turned me into someone willing to risk it all for something that really hadn't been worth risking.

During this past week since Marcus had been gone, I'd had some really sad moments when I'd wished I had never won the lottery money. If I hadn't, I wouldn't have been able to afford the surgery and Marcus wouldn't have left me. He would have had no reason. I wouldn't have had to tell a lie about going to the game because I knew that if it hadn't been for my weight loss, Antonio would have never given me a second glance.

But now I was smack dab in the middle of a game I no longer knew if I really wanted to play.

So, you just lost Marcus for nothing?

That little voice in my head that kept asking that question finally made me erase all doubt. I'd made this bed, so I needed to lay in it. And no better to person to lay in it with than Antonio.

I sprayed some perfume behind both of my ears, then I went down the front of my body. I noted some areas I was going to have to have even more lipo in, but this three-hundred dollar lingerie tucked everything in in just the right places, so for now, I knew he'd approve of my outfit.

I fought back the uneasy feeling in my gut. Part of me just wanted to sit in a corner and cry over Marcus, but I needed Antonio. Being with him was the only thing that would heal my hurting heart.

"Yep, this is gonna be good for us both," I told myself all the way to his house.

Chapter 26

Terrance

I was back in front of the building I swore I'd never set foot in again – trying to set foot in it. But the Hulk Hogan security guard wasn't having it.

"Come on, Dante. Let me in," I said. "I just need to talk to my wife."

Dante stroked his goatee. "Yo, let me see. What were your words after you told Mr. Perry to kiss your crack. Oh, yeah. 'I'm rich, bitch'. And if I remember correctly, you told me to 'keep working my minimum wage job and pumping my steroids and maybe one day I could come work for you'. Weren't those your exact words?"

"I, ah, I ah. . . " I didn't know what to say. I had gone out like a champ. The day after we returned from Austin, I came up to the job and showed out. That wasn't even my nature, but it was funny how money gave you juice you never had before.

"I, ah, I ah," he said, mimicking me. "Yeah, those were the exact words."

I glanced around at many of my co-workers, who were no doubt heading back from lunch and now wondering what I was doing back here. "I need to see my wife."

Dante laughed at that. "Oh, no I heard you were so full of yourself that your wife was the second thing you dumped after your job."

My first instinct was to cuss him out, but since I needed something from him, I said, "Look, brother."

"Nah, you look, *brother*. Since I want to keep my *minimum wage* job, I'm not gonna stomp you right now, but I am gonna tell you to get off these premises." He pulled out his cell phone. "Or, I'm calling the cops."

I recognized one of Sheray's coworkers headed toward the elevator, so I yelled, "Martina, can you get Sheray? Tell her I'm down here and need to talk to her. Please?"

Since that embarrassing day at the restaurant I had literally been pining for my wife. I didn't want to date. I didn't want to party. I just wanted Sheray. And since she wouldn't take my calls and I had no idea where she was staying, my only option was to come to the job. "Please, Martina!" I called out again.

Martina rolled her eyes at me and stepped on the elevator.

Dante moved closer to me and lowered his voice, "Dude, don't make me sucker punch you in front of all these white people."

"I don't want any trouble. I just want to talk to my wife." I couldn't believe that I was doing this. But my heart was aching for Sheray. I'd messed up and I'd do whatever I had to do to make it right. "Son, move out of the way." I pushed Dante. Of course, his 350-pound frame didn't budge. But he did grab me and pull me into a chokehold.

"You know," Dante said, as my arms flailed around and I struggled to break free, "this is so not a good look for a millionaire bachelor."

I had to pause at those words. I held my hands up. "Okay, okay, man. I'm cool."

He paused to make sure that I was calm, then he slowly loosened his grip, and when he saw that I wasn't going to fight, he pushed me away. "Dawg, if the money got you buggin' out like that, I don't even want it."

I ran my hand over my face. Why was I bugging out? I was the one that wanted out. I was the one that didn't want to be married. She was giving me what I wanted – my single life back, so why was I dying to see her?

"Go home, Terrance," Dante said.

I was just about to sulk away in defeat when I saw my wife step off the elevator. I must've been a sad sight as I stared hopefully at her.

"Terrance, what are you doing?" she asked as she approached me.

Dante had the nerve to step protectively in front of her.

"It's okay, Dante. He won't hurt me. At least not physically. He can't break my heart any more than he already has."

Those words tore at my heart.

"I need to talk to you. Baby, I'm so sorry. I need you. Please come back to me," I said, reaching for her.

For once, I didn't care who saw me. I didn't care who thought I was weak. Since that day in the restaurant two weeks ago, I hadn't been able to function. I had no idea how much I loved Sheray – until she was gone. There truly was nothing like absence to make you miss someone's presence.

"What do you want from me?" she asked, pointedly.

"I want you back."

"Go home, Terrance."

She said it but the way her voice quivered, I knew that it wasn't what she truly wanted.

"Not until you forgive me and come back home," I said.

"Come back home? For what? You made it very clear that you don't want to be married."

"The only thing I made clear is that I'm a fool," I replied. "I don't feel whole anymore. I miss everything about you, your smile, your touch, your quoting Steve Harvey." I expected her to laugh. She didn't, but I seized the silence and stepped forward.

' "Please, Baby. Please forgive me and take me back."

As a slow tear slid down her cheek, she said, "You really hurt me."

"And let me spend the rest of my life making it up to you," I said, pulling her close to me.

She looked around and I guess the number of people all up in our business made her uncomfortable because she slowly exhaled, backed away, then said, "Go home, Terrance." Before I could protest, she held up her hand. "I'll come by after I get off from work."

"That's just it, Baby, you don't have to work. We're rich," I said, for the first time truly acknowledging that my money was her money.

"*You're* rich. I'm not. Our marriage is getting annulled, which means we were never legally married, which means I'm not entitled to your money."

"Girl, don't be no fool," Dante mumbled.

I threw up my hands as if to say 'Really?'

He shrugged and stepped back.

"It's too late for an annulment. We only had thirty days," I told her, feeling a glimmer of hope.

She folded her arms. "Then, I'll begin the paperwork for a divorce tomorrow."

The mention of the word 'divorce' felt like a sledgehammer being slammed into my stomach.

"I should have done it already," she said, looking like she was silently chastising herself.

The fact that she hadn't filed meant there was still hope. I seized the opportunity and stepped closer. "You haven't because that's not what you really want. It's not what I want. I was a fool, Baby. The money doesn't matter if you don't have someone to share it with."

"I'm sure there's no shortage of people for you to share it with."

"I want the right person to share it with. I want you."

"I told you, I didn't care about the money, I cared about you." She sighed again. "Just go home and we'll talk later, okay?"

I wanted to protest some more, but I finally just said, "So you'll come by after work?"

"Yes."

"Will you bring your stuff?"

She hesitated. "Maybe."

That made me break out into a huge grin. Right now, maybe would have to do.

Chapter 27

Janine

Owen had made good on his threat. That's the only thing that could explain why Tony was sitting in our living room, playing with our son like we were one big happy family.

Tony had shown up just as William was coming home from school. I knew it was all planned because the minute my son saw him, he lit up. Tony had only been to see William twice since he moved out. Oh, he'd made promises, but they always ended up broken because "something came up." But the way my son was acting – like a kid on Christmas – none of that mattered now.

Despite my attempts to get Tony to wrap up his visit and leave, he continued to ignore me and pretend that we were fine. My son was over-the-moon ecstatic and that's the only reason I didn't cuss Tony out, as I was kicking him out.

"Son, it's eight-thirty. Time for bed," I finally said. William was sitting on the sofa, showing his dad some videos on his phone.

"Awww, Ma. . ."

"Don't awww, Ma me."

He turned to Tony. "Daddy, can't you stay, please?"

Tony looked at me with puppy dog eyes and it made my stomach turn. "I'd love to stay, son, but I don't think your mom will let me."

"Mom, please?" William said, jumping up and down. I wanted to slap my soon-to-be-ex.

"Goodnight, son."

The tone of my voice let him know this wasn't open for discussion. He stuck out his bottom lip as Tony took him in his arms.

"I love you, son. I'll be back."

I could tell William was trying hard to fight back tears and it broke my heart. I was so angry, I had to grind my teeth to keep from going off.

"I love that little boy," Tony said as soon as William was gone. He took a step toward me. "I love my wife, too."

I moved away from him. "You don't have a wife. You left, remember?" I turned and walked into the kitchen and he followed behind me. "How's the Pop Tart working out for you?" I felt compelled to ask.

"She's not. We broke up." He leaned up against the kitchen counter.

"Cry me a freakin' river." I removed a glass from the rack, put it in the cabinet and slammed the door shut. I was trying to busy myself to keep my cool.

"She's just on the go all the time, I can't keep up," he said like I really cared.

"She's twenty-one, you're forty-one. What did you expect?"

He didn't answer and instead watched me put away the dishes. "I miss this. I miss our family," he said after a few minutes. "Can we talk about working this out?"

This fool wasn't fooling anyone. I barely heard from him and now he wanted me to act like we were fine? "No, we can't work anything out. The only thing I want to talk to you about is when you plan to see your son. This staying out of his life, then popping back in isn't good for him."

"William was happy to see me." He stepped toward me again. "What about you? Were you happy to see me?"

I tossed the plate I was holding down on the counter. "Really, Tony?"

"So, you're just going to stay mad?" he asked.

"Are you serious?" He was really trying me. I was already freaking out behind Darnell. Now I had to listen to this foolishness. "Tony, you left me to go be with your twenty-one-year-old kickboxing instructor. I'm not mad, I'm pissed and I have no words for you."

The smile left his face and he stared at me. "You know, you never asked me why."

"What?" I replied, exasperated.

"You never asked me why I left," he repeated, walking over to take a seat at the kitchen table.

"I know why," I snapped. "You lost interest in our marriage when the Pop Tart came along."

He shook his head. "No, our marriage was dying long before she was in the picture. I felt like we were going in two different directions. And every time I tried to talk to you about it, you wanted to bury your head. You don't like to deal with issues until it's too late. So, yeah, I lost interest because I was unhappy. I lost interest because you didn't support me."

I threw up my hands. "What are you talking about?"

He had the audacity to look offended. "I'm talking about my dreams. You never have supported my dream to get into the music industry. You were content with me working at the post office for the rest of my life, despite how miserable it made me. I felt resentful and you never noticed or cared."

I slammed my palm on the kitchen table. "You want to be a freakin' rapper, Tony! And let me repeat myself, you're forty-one. There is a cap-out age for rapping as a serious profession."

His lips tightened and I could tell he was struggling to contain his anger. "LL still raps. Ice Cube still raps."

"In their *spare time*!" I yelled. "When they're not making movies and TV shows. And they didn't *start* their rap careers in their forties!"

The way his chest heaved up and down, I could tell he was serious and that floored me.

"Joel Osteen says its never too late to follow your dreams."

Was he really quoting TV preachers now?

"Joel Osteen also makes $2,334,000 a minute. He can say whatever he wants." I took a deep breath. I didn't know why I was even entertaining this foolishness. "Do you hear yourself? You have a family and you fail to realize that comes with some responsibility. You think I wanted to go up to Clearcast and get cussed out by folks on a daily basis? No, but I did it because we have a little boy in there that depended on us to put a roof over his head and clothes on his back."

"But I knew you were unhappy and I encouraged you to go back to school, find another job. But you didn't want to better yourself. You were content wallowing in your discontent and you were bringing me down with you. I just couldn't take it anymore."

Now he sounded exasperated. "All I wanted was someone to believe in me."

I was tired of this discussion. Our relationship was done, so we didn't even need to pretend otherwise

"Tony, why are you even here?" I asked. When he'd first arrived, I just knew it was because Owen had opened his big mouth Now, I wasn't so sure.

He stared at me. "You know, I was hoping that we could talk but with you, that's virtually impossible. So, yeah, I'll cut straight to the chase. Did you win some money that you're trying to hide from me?"

I returned his stare. And there it was.

"And before you get ready to lie," he continued, "I spoke with Owen. Now, I'm going to ask you again."

I had no idea what to say or how to handle this, which was crazy because I knew that this day was coming. Maybe Tony was right, I didn't like dealing with issues until they were staring me in the face.

Tony leaned back in his seat. "Owen told me that you actually had Darnell claim the money. So I know you think I'm slow, but I did a little homework before I came here. Word on the street is that Darnell is living the life."

"Darnell won the lottery. I didn't," I said, my tone defiant.

"Oh, so Darnell played the lotto with your coworkers? Okay." He nodded as he slowly stood. "You know what? I messed up, I did. I'm sorry. But your hatred for me just messed you up. Believe that." He moved toward the door. "You'll be hearing from my attorney. And soon."

As my husband walked out of our home, I knew he was right. I was going to pay for trying to cheat him, he'd see to that. The question now was, just how bad was this story going to end?

Chapter 28

Angelique

I squinted and did my best to peer through the blinds of the sidelights on Antonio's front porch. I'd already rang the doorbell three times and Antonio hadn't answered. The beveled glass of the front door distorted my view, but I could see that the television was on.

He knew I was on my way, so why in the world wasn't he answering the door?

I pressed the lit-up circle once again, and finally, I heard the speakers on the intercom.

"Yeah? Who is it?"

A wide smile spread across my face. Then, I cleared my throat in an attempt to sound less enthused than I was. "Hey, Baby. It's me."

I heard the phone hang up and shortly after that the door swung open.

Antonio wore a pair of sweats that hung off of his waist just low enough so I could see the bottom of his stomach. The parts that were covered, I'd see soon enough. There were small beads of water trickling down his chest and he had a white bath towel draped around his neck. I could smell the scent of soap even though we stood about two feet away from one another.

"I thought you'd changed your mind," he said with a wicked grin.

My heart warmed in anticipation. It wasn't just my imagination. He did seem more excited than normal to see me.

"I just stopped at home to slip into this," I said, pulling the strap on my coat so that it would open. His eyes lit up and he smiled his approval at my attire. He took my arm and pulled me inside.

"Dang, girl, I missed you," he said, closing his door.

"I missed you, too."

He continued leading me toward the stairs that led to his bedroom. Dang, he wasn't wasting any time.

"We were just getting started," he said.

That caused me to stop with my stiletto mid-air. I pulled my hand away and stepped back. *"We?"*

Just then, a gorgeous young woman descended down the stairs. She looked like she'd stepped right out of a rap video with her exotic features and long jet-black hair. She was wearing a black lace bra and a matching lace thong.

I was speechless as I watched her. And I couldn't help but notice how Antonio was watching her, too. I saw his manhood rise as she slowly made her way over to me.

"Ooooh, Babe, you were right," the woman said as she ran her hands over my cheek, "she is cute."

Her touch snapped me out of my daze and caused me to jerk my head away from her. The woman giggled as her eyes roamed up and down my body. She placed her hand on my thigh. "She's a little flabby, though. Like she used to be fat and lost a lot of weight."

I gasped and knocked her hand away. A look of disgust crept up on Antonio's face. "You used to be fat?"

I was too much in shock to speak so the girl spoke up. "It's okay, though, Babe. I can work with this."

I wanted to cry. Antonio was looking at me like he was trying to imagine me fat. I had never been so humiliated in my life.

"Wh-what's going on?" I asked Antonio, finally finding my voice. "Why did you tell me to come over?"

He shook off his apprehension. "To join the party," he said. He glanced over at the woman, who was feeling herself up right in the middle of his foyer. "So, what's up?" Antonio asked. "You in? Diamond has a mean tongue."

That chick had the nerve to wiggle her tongue in my direction. In all my life, I had never felt so low. I didn't say a word and just turned and bolted toward the door.

"Come on, Baby, you're gonna miss the fun!" Diamond called out after me.

I was almost to my car by the time Antonio caught up with me.

"What's up? Why are you trippin'?" he asked.

I looked at him like he'd lost his mind. "Are you serious? You invite me over and I think it's because you want to be with me and I find out it's because you want a threesome?"

"And the problem would be? Shoot, I thought you'd be down."

"Why would you think that?"

It was his turn to look at me crazy. "Umm, let's see. . . we had sex on the first date, the second date and every date after that. Matter of fact, we haven't even had a *date*, we just had sex."

Okay, so I was wrong. *This* was the lowest I ever felt. Mainly because he was right. It hadn't even registered with me that Antonio hadn't taken me anywhere. Other than the game, I hadn't even seen him outside of a bedroom.

"I. . . I just thought, I mean. . ."

"Look, if you're not cool with a sexual relationship, because that's all I'm looking for, then we might need to chill, for real. I told you from jump, I'm not looking to get serious and when I am ready to settle down. . . well, it'll be with a different type of woman."

I didn't know what that meant, and I was too hurt to ask. "Wow," was all I could manage to say.

"Sorry." He shrugged. "It is what it is. See you around."

He didn't even wait for me to get in my car. He just turned around and walked back into the house. I wasted no time jumping into my car, putting it in reverse, and screeching out of the driveway, barely making it to the corner before the tears came tumbling down.

Chapter 29

Raquelle

If I hadn't been a believer before, I was definitely one now. God was the only explanation as to why my son was sitting in my living room, giggling at his sister as she tried to play Sony PlayStation. He'd been home a week and his recovery had been almost miraculous. He still had a long battle ahead, but the first 48 hours after a kidney transplant are the most crucial and my son had come through like a champ. I'd never been so happy.

Today, however, my happiness would be short-lived as I was on my way for a one-on-one with Mr. Perry. We had a court date on Monday and my attorney had urged me to stay away from Mr. Perry until then. But I was a mother who needed to mother. So I was grateful that Elsa had convinced him to meet with me. Now, I planned on doing whatever it took to get Mr. Perry to drop the charges.

I made my way back into my bedroom to finish preparing for my meeting with Mr. Perry. My mother appeared in my doorway. "Why are you wearing that low cut dress with your boobs all propped up?"

"I don't know," I said. Honestly, the fuchsia wrap dress made me uncomfortable, but if Mr. Perry's wandering eye could convince him to take my offer, then it was worth it.

"I know why," my mother said. "Breasts have weakened many a men, so whatever works. Here." She held out her hand toward me.

"What is this?" I asked, taking the item she was holding.

"It's Tiana's volleyball kneepads. Because if you need to get down on your knees and beg that man, or whatever else you need to do, you need to do it, so he can drop these charges."

I tossed the kneepads on my bed. "First of all, that's disgusting, mother."

She shook her head as she walked in my room. "You're the one whose mind went straight to the gutter. I was talking about getting on your knees to pray."

"Oh," I replied, chuckling.

"And the way your boobs are sitting up like they're ready to do a salute, don't act like you're above using your womanly wiles." She chuckled. "But, baby, you have to do whatever it takes. Your son has been given a new lease on life."

My mother was so right. And now, I needed one, too.

My attorney said that a jury would probably sympathize with me and give me probation, but it was that 'probably' part that I wasn't willing to gamble on. Even if I only had to do two years, which the attorney said he thought I'd get if I was found guilty, that was too long.

I walked into the living room, kissed Shaun and Tiana on the forehead. "Okay, take care of my babies. Hopefully, I'll have some good news when I get back."

Neither Shaun nor Tiana had any idea what was going on with me professionally and I prayed they never had to find out.

I drove in silence to the Clearcast building, stressed beyond belief and praying the entire way. I ignored the looks of the people at the front desk and the coworkers I passed in the hall. Mr. Perry's secretary greeted me, the expression on her face a mixture of pity and disgust.

"You can go in," she said.

"Thank you." I took a deep breath and pushed back my nervousness. I would beg, plead, whatever I had to do.

Mr. Perry sat at the head of the table. His attorney, Mr. Lyons, sat to the right of him.

"Mrs. Vargas," Mr. Lyons said, nodding in my direction.

"Hello, Mr. Lyons." I slid into a seat on the other end of the table. "Good afternoon, Mr. Perry."

He all but snarled in my direction.

"Well, I have been talking with Mr. Perry and trying to work out something. But quite frankly, Mr. Perry isn't interested in any deals," Mr. Lyons began.

I jumped right in. "Mr. Perry, I know what I did was wrong and I can give you the whys all day. But there is no justification for my behavior."

"You're absolutely right," he said. "Two things I can't stand, a liar and a thief and you are both of those."

He'd said that to me the day I was fired, but I guess he felt the need to repeat himself. "You are right," I replied. "But I'm just pleading with you. Is there any way I can make this right with you?"

"Yes, you can serve your time for being a thief," he said, matter-of-factly.

I took a deep breath. "Is there any other way? My son just came through his kidney transplant."

He stiffened and I seized the moment.

"I know you have a son. You're very proud of him, as you should be. But if he were in a position where he needed you to ease his pain, I'm assuming you'd go to great lengths to do what you needed to do, even if that included something that was totally out of character for you," I said.

"Don't try to turn this around," Mr. Perry said, leaning forward onto the table. "Even if I gave you the benefit of the doubt about the surgery, I checked you out." He looked down at a piece of paper in front of him. "This wasn't all about your son. A new car, a new house, designer clothes, and purses. That sounds like greed to me, not motherly concern."

I cringed inside. He was right about that and I didn't have a good feeling when I broke down and bought those Jimmy Choo shoes and matching bag, but I'd never in my life had anything nice and I just wanted to do something for me.

"It's been so hard raising my children alone and I just wanted. . . "

"There are lots of single mothers out there who don't turn into thieves."

I had no words, no justification, so I figured I would just return to begging. "I can spend my lifetime making this up to you. I can pay back triple, quadruple the amount I took, just please don't send me to jail," I pleaded.

"Don't you get it? This isn't about the money. This is about the principle of what you did." He leaned back. "But I'm not as cold-hearted as you may think."

My heart fluttered as he glanced over at his attorney, who pulled out a legal sized document from his briefcase.

"Mr. Perry understands that you are a single mother and so he has considered your pleas," Mr. Lyons said.

"And?" I said with baited breath.

"And he may be willing to entertain the idea of working something out."

"Oh, my God," I said, clutching both hands in front of me. "Whatever I need to do, I'll do it."

My heart was racing as the attorney continued, "In light of your recent instant millionaire status, Mr. Perry would be willing to drop the charges in exchange for your lottery winnings."

I wanted to do a dance. "Of course. How much?"

"All of it."

My heart was no longer fluttering. It had plummeted into my small intestines.

"Wh-what?"

"According to our investigators, you've had your son's surgery and even paid for his care for several years."

"Yes, but. . . "

"Then, what's the problem? We'll take all that's left." He glanced down at the documents. "All $6,830,000, give or take a few dollars. We'll leave you with enough to cover your rent and utilities for the next six months. That should give you enough time to find another job. We've drawn up the paperwork for you sign everything over to Mr. Perry."

"Th-this is extortion," I stammered.

"I prefer to call it fair trade," Mr. Perry said, smirking.

"Technically, it's not extortion," the attorney said. "You stole from Mr. Perry. The interest he is charging in order to honor your request to make this disappear, totals $6,830,000. He's being quite generous if you ask me. It all boils down to how much your freedom is worth to you."

"Call it your penance. With interest," Mr. Perry added.

"Give him *everything*?" I mumbled. *Maybe I should take my chances in court*, I thought.

As if he was reading my mind, Mr. Lyons said, "Let me be very clear. We know you can hire the best attorneys now, but so can we. And embezzlement is a crime punishable by up to seventy years in prison. Even if you lucked up and only got ten years in prison, your little Shaun will be what, nineteen when you get out? And Heaven forbid, he should relapse and you aren't there for him. Your teenaged daughter will probably be so devastated and embarrassed by all the media coverage – because there will be media coverage – that she'll run into the arms of the first little boy that makes her feel good. Since you'll be locked up, you won't be able to protect her and well, she'll end up just another statistic. Is that a chance you want to take?"

He had some valid points. My kids were the most important part of this equation. Mr. Perry just sat there with that stupid smirk across his face. I didn't know what to do but I knew that my freedom was priceless. I needed that money, but then I remembered my mother's words: *God has already given you the means to save your son's life.* And I'd done that. I'd saved my son's life. Now, God was giving me a way to save my own.

Mr. Perry smiled as I picked up the pen and pulled the paper toward me. "Where do I sign?"

Chapter 30

Angelique

Three weeks and five days.

That's how long it took me to catch up with Marcus and convince him to meet with me. He refused to come to the house, so we decided to meet at Starbucks at 10 a.m.

I'd had a lot of time to think, and I knew without a doubt that Marcus was the man for me. I hadn't heard from Antonio since the night I'd left his house, not that I even wanted to. I erased his phone number from my contacts and vowed that I would never again put myself in a position where someone saw me as nothing more than a sidepiece. I'd lost my man for a man that saw no value in me. That's why I was determined to win Marcus back.

I made a point to arrive fifteen minutes early to ensure I'd be there before him. I ordered two green teas for us and sat down at a table. Marcus walked in and spotted me right away. I stood up and gave him a hug.

"It's so good to see you," I said as I let go and sat back down.

He smiled. "Same here. You look beautiful as usual."

I could feel myself blushing. I'd purposely won a royal blue dress that was a deep contrast to my caramel skin. It hugged me in all the right places. I'd just left the beauty shop so my hair was tight. I just wanted Marcus to see what he was missing.

"Thank you. I'm sure I don't have to tell you how handsome you look." I slid his drink to him. "I bought you a green tea."

"That was nice of you. Thanks." He took a sip of his tea and looked at me.

"No. Thank you for agreeing to meet with me this morning. I didn't think you were ever going to speak to me again." I shook my head. "I want you to know how terribly sorry I am for treating you the way I did." I pinched the bridge of my nose and closed my eyes. "I feel like an idiot for allowing you to walk out of my life."

He patted my hand.

"Hey, don't be so down on yourself. You were going through a lot and I know it was hard to make those adjustments. I just couldn't understand why you didn't see that my love for you was real."

"I realize that now. I have also come to realize that I want us to be together. No more lies and deceit. I promise this time I am going to be the woman you want and need." I smiled at him. He didn't smile back. In fact, the look on his face told me that he wasn't going to be so easily convinced. I reached across the table and rubbed his hand. "Marcus, are you listening?"

"Uh, yeah. I'm listening. This is just a lot to take in." He tapped the tabletop a few times then he rubbed his chin.

"I understand. I shouldn't have expected you to just accept my apology like nothing ever happened. It's going to take some time for us to rebuild our relationship." I paused, then continued, "But, you know what? If any two people can do it, it's us. I love you, Marcus."

Marcus sat silently. He looked away from me and shook his head. When he looked at me again, he said, "I accept your apology and I love you, too."

I paused, then said, "Why do I feel a 'but' coming on?"

He took a deep breath.

"Because there is a 'but'. I accept your apology and I love you, too *but* I think it's best that we remain apart. As much as I hate to admit it, I don't feel that I'll ever be able to trust you completely again."

I slid my cup back and forth on the table as I thought of what to say. "So, you're not even willing to give us another chance?"

I didn't want to cry, but I hadn't been able to smile these past four weeks. I'd shopped. I'd done the spa thing. I'd lived life to the fullest. And I'd never felt more miserable.

"Angelique," he said, "not only did you lie to me, you brushed me off. How do you think that made me feel? I'm sorry, but I feel that chapter of our lives has ended."

I could feel my throat tightening up. "So this is it? You're just gonna leave me?"

"You left me. When you decided to pursue a relationship with another man, you gave up on me."

"I just . . . I mean he made me feel beautiful." I didn't know what else to say.

"And I didn't?" has asked dumbfounded.

"I showered you with compliments *before* your surgery and after. I loved Angelique. Not heavy Angelique. Not thin Angelique. Just Angelique. And it wasn't good enough."

He sighed. "There's nothing left to say. I will always love you and have a place for you in my heart." This time, it was he who reached across the table for my hand. He gave it a squeeze, kissed it, and then he stood up. "You take care."

And just like that, he was gone. I always thought if I had money, all of my problems would be solved. But, instead, I ended up with more problems than I ever bargained for. The best things in life really are free. And love? Well, that's invaluable.

Chapter 31

Terrance

I had never been so happy to see my wife. But what made me even happier was seeing what was in her hand.

"Let me take your suitcase," I said, taking the leather rolling case out of her hand before she changed her mind.

She walked in and her eyes lit up at the four-course meal laid out on the table, and the chef standing at the head waiting to greet her.

"Madame," the chef said.

"Good evening." Sheray turned to me. "What is all of this?"

"It's just the first step in my trying to make things right with you." I reached to try and pull her toward me, but she pushed away.

"Terrance, it's not that easy."

I was hurt, but not deterred. Of course, I wished there was a way I could wave a magic wand and get her back. "If you didn't want to marry me, then you shouldn't have asked," she said.

I turned to the chef. I'd had to pay triple to get this last minute favor from one of the top chefs in town. But I was ready to win back my wife.

"Excuse us, we'll be ready for dinner in a little bit." The chef nodded and eased back into the kitchen. I took Sheray's hand and led her back into the living room.

"You know how much I love you," I said, once we sat down on the sofa. "It was just something about marriage that scared me and then, things just happened so fast."

"But you proposed to me."

She was right about that. But when I asked her, I meant it, I wanted to marry her. . . only I was talking about two or four years from then. But I didn't want to make things worse, so I simply said, "And I meant it. It was just all so overwhelming to me. But these past few months have shown me more than anything, I don't want to live without you."

A slow tear slid down her cheek. "All I ever wanted to do was love you."

I wiped her face. "And I am so sorry, baby. I promise, you never have to worry about me being a jerk again. I mean, I may leave the toilet seat up. I may even get moody from time to time. But I will never let you go."

"What happened to your bachelor life?"

"It's not all that it's cut out to be."

She raised an eyebrow. "So you dabbled in it?"

I weighed my words. I was determined to make things right with Sheray and honesty was a huge part of that. But if I told her about the women I'd been with since our breakup, she would grab her bag and march right back out that door.

"No, I just hung out, kicked it."

"Kicked it? What does that mean? I mean, I figured you were out enjoying your bachelor life, hanging out and stuff, but. . . you are still married and I just thought. . . I prayed you placed some value on that." Her voice stiffened and a lie inched toward the end of my tongue. Sheray wasn't dumb. I'm sure deep down inside, she knew better, but there was a difference between thinking and knowing for sure. And if I admitted the women that I'd slept with, she'd *know* and wouldn't be able to move past that.

"I've thought about this a lot," she continued, her eyes filling with moisture, "and I'm like Sheray, don't be a fool, but," she turned and stared at me, "you've already hurt me so bad and it's gonna be hard enough getting over that. So, part of me wants to know if you've slept with other women, but the other part needs something to hang onto, some belief that you didn't completely abandon our marriage."

I would never understand why women didn't get that for some men, sex was just that, sex. My sleeping with other women in no way diminished how I felt about Sheray. But staring at my wife, I knew that nothing I said would convince her of that. So when I looked into her eyes, the lie that I had pushed back earlier, found its way out.

"I didn't abandon our marriage. I haven't had sex with anyone else. I needed to figure out what was going to happen with us first," I said. The lie pinched my heart. I really wanted to be open and honest, but I knew Sheray, and there was no way she'd be able to handle news about one woman, let alone the many I'd been with.

A beat, then, "So, you haven't slept with anyone else?"

I forced a reassuring smile. "I haven't."

Her shoulders sank in relief, like she'd been praying for that answer. I didn't know whether she really believed it or if she just wanted to believe it so bad. Either way, all I knew was I was about to seize my second chance.

"I was hanging out. But I'm committed to you. I only want you. That part of our marriage is still sacred." I felt awful about lying, but we were just getting back to a good place. As far as I was concerned, I was ready to erase the last few months from my memory as if they never happened. She slowly took my hand. "I love you, Terrance."

"I love you, too, Sheray."

We stared into each other's eyes before I leaned in and our lips met. The kiss on her lips led to one on her neck, then her shoulder. Her moans were my permission to continue. It was as if her body was crying out in relief.

"What about the chef?" she panted.

"He's fine," I said, standing and leading her into the bedroom, where I spent the next hour showing her just how happy I was to have her home.

After our dessert of lovemaking, we made it into the kitchen for dinner. The chef had prepared mesquite salmon, truffle asparagus, and crescents. We were just about to dig into our raspberry soufflé when the doorbell rang.

"You expecting someone?" she asked.

"No," I said. I stood and made my way to the door. I glanced out the peephole and my heart dropped.

I was about to turn and race back into the dining room when the woman on the other side started banging on the door. "I see you're in there," she shouted. "I see your eyeball, Terrance."

Sheray appeared in the living room, her arms folded. I knew immediately our night was ruined.

"Open up, Mr. Big Shot!"

"I-It's, I. . ."

Sheray didn't bother waiting on me to fumble through an explanation. She pushed past me and swung the door open.

I didn't know whether to cry at the timing, or strangle the woman standing at my front door. It was Mia, the woman that had robbed me. How would I explain that to my wife? It's obvious she wasn't expecting to see Sheray.

"May I help you?" Sheray said.

Mia smacked her lips, then put her hands on her hips. "You can help me by telling Terrance I need to talk to him."

Sheray stepped aside and motioned for her to come in. "Come on in so we can all talk."

Mia pushed past Sheray and stormed into my house. I would deal with explaining things to Sheray later, but right now, I was two seconds from doing something my mother had taught me never to do – knock the mess out of a woman.

"Have you lost your mind?" I asked her.

This chick had the nerve to smile seductively. "Nope, how are you, baby?"

"What the hell is wrong with you? What are you doing at my house?" I demanded.

She ran a finger along the side of my cheek. I grabbed her arm and flung it away. "Oh, so it's like that now?"

"Who are you?" Sheray asked.

Mia looked at her, smirked, but didn't reply as she turned back to me.

Sheray spun around and started walking toward the bedroom. "You know what," she said to me, her voice shaking, "you look like you got some things to take care of, so I'm gonna get my stuff and go."

"Yeah, why don't you do that?" Mia sneered. "I have some things I need to discuss with Terry."

"Sheray!" I said, grabbing her arm just as she passed me. "You are not leaving. You are my wife and you're going to let me explain this."

"Your wife?" Mia snapped. "Oh, where was your wife when you were laid up with me?"

That took the air out of Sheray's body and she jerked free. "You had sex with her?"

"Girl, sex is an understatement," Mia moaned, running her hands down her body like she was savoring the memory. "He sexed me up, down and all around the room." She pointed all around the room.

"You made love to her in our house?" Sheray exclaimed.

"No!" I replied. "I didn't bring her to our house. I met her at a club. . ."

"But you did sleep with her?" Sheray's glare was accusing and before I could try to clean up my words, Mia stepped up and draped her arm through mine.

"And he left me with a little gift," she purred as she tried to take my hand.

Sheray stared at me with complete disdain and my heart crumbled. I jerked my hand away from Mia and stepped toward Sheray. "Baby, I'm sorry. It didn't mean anything. It was one time. This chick stole my money and my clothes and I haven't heard from her since."

Mia had the nerve to laugh as she plopped down in my recliner. "Sorry about that, Boo. It's what I do." She grinned at me. "Or what I *used* to do before I found out my baby daddy had hit the lotto."

Both Sheray and I did a double take.

"Who-what did you say?" Sheray asked.

"Terry is gonna - "

"Terrance, my name is Terrance," I screamed.

"Sorry," she chuckled. "We didn't spend much time talking. But like I said, you did leave me a little gift." She patted her stomach. "We're having a baby!" she announced like it was the best news ever. I guess for her, it was.

"B-but . . ." I couldn't find my breath, let alone manage any words.

"But we used a condom?" She laughed. "You had two, genius, but we did it three times, remember." She looked at Sheray. "It was a very long night."

This time, Sheray didn't bother going to get her stuff. She just snatched her purse off the counter and bolted out the door. I would've gone after her but I was literally too stunned to move.

Mia, who obviously was finding this all very amusing, looked around the house. "So, where are we gonna put the crib?" she asked.

"Get out," I managed to say.

"What?"

"I. Said. Get. Out."

She shrugged like it was no big deal then stood up. "Look, I know we got off to a bad start and all, but we're stuck for the next eighteen years. And I don't expect you to believe this kid is yours but the other dude I was with that week was snipped. So," she patted my shoulder, "congratulations. Let me know when you're ready for the DNA test. I'd be glad to prove it to you." She headed toward the door. "See you soon." Then she walked out singing "I'm rich, Trick," by rapper Lil Jon.

Chapter 32

Janine

I didn't recognize the number that had shown up on my Caller ID. I didn't want to answer it because I was scared it might be Tony calling from an anonymous number saying that he was suing me. I thought about trying to make a deal with him, but my pride wouldn't let me. Besides, I had to get the money back first. And since it had been two weeks since I had talked to Darnell, I was beginning to wonder if that was even possible.

The phone, which had stopped ringing, started again and the same strange number popped up. It dawned on me that it might be Darnell calling me from a different phone, so I quickly answered.

"Hello?"

"Janine?"

"Yes?" I didn't recognize the female caller.

"This LaQuanta, Darnell's girlfriend."

"Do you know where he is?" I asked, not bothering with small talk.

"That's why I'm calling you." Her voice sounded panicked. "Darnell is in trouble."

That made me sit up in my seat at my dining room table, where I'd been parked at my laptop, stalking Darnell's FB trying to find an indication of where he was. But my cousin wasn't social media savvy and so all I'd seen were a lot of game requests. "What kind of trouble is he in? Is he okay?"

"Ah, no," she replied. "He, umm . . . he needs you."

"Needs me to do what?"

She paused. I could tell by her hesitation that she didn't want to continue.

"LaQuanta, would you just tell me what is going on?" I said.

"I told Darnell that he should just let me do it."

"Do what?"

She sighed. "Darnell owes these dudes some money."

I rolled my eyes. Of course she'd be all extra over something as simple as that. "Okay? I'm sure he told you that he has some money."

She clicked her teeth. "Yeah, he told me. He even bought me a new car, a Hyundai. I don't know why I couldn't get the Benz I wanted, but I guess its better than nothing."

Oh yeah, as soon as I hooked up with Darnell, I was withdrawing that money.

"But look," she continued, "they got him."

"What?"

"Man-man and Tank got him."

"Who is Man-man and Tank?" I asked.

"They work for Fat Freddy."

"Who the hell is Fat Freddy?"

"He's the dude Darnell owes the money to," she said, like I was supposed to know that.

I took a deep breath and reminded myself that I was dealing with a simple chick. "Okay, well, why doesn't Darnell just pay him what he owes them?"

"Well, you know Darnell got a mouth on him and he started talking smack and he told him about all the money he had access to and they, well, they kinda holding him hostage."

"Hostage?" I screamed.

"Yeah. He said for you to go to his mama's house and go out to the storage shed. There's a loose panel against the back wall. He has $800-thousand there. I would've gone to get the money, but you know your auntie don't like me."

I wanted to let LaQuanta know that my aunt wasn't the only one who didn't like her, but instead, I just said, "So, he's hiding my money in his mama's house?"

"Look, he can explain it all to you later. He said it's $800 g's there. He needs you to get five for Man-Man and Tank, and leave the other three there."

I couldn't believe Darnell had stashed almost a million dollars in a storage shed.

"Then what am I supposed to do once I get the money?"

"Swing by here and get me, then we gotta take the money to Fat Freddy."

I wanted to scream. "Fine, text me your address." I hung up, then quickly dialed my neighbor to ask her to keep an eye out for William who was due home from school any minute.

Ten minutes later, I was in my car, speeding to my Aunt Ora's house.

"Hey, baby. What you doing back?" she asked after I banged on her front door. "And why you banging like you done lost your mind?"

"Darnell wants me to get something in the storage shed out back."

"The storage shed?"

"Yes."

"Where is he? When did he get back? You remind him that I can't miss my doctor's appointment Thursday?

These cataracts are getting worse. Today, I thought they'd brought Ricardo Montalban back to Family Feud. Turns out it was just Steve Harvey."

"All right, Auntie," I said, trying to scurry past her. Luckily, she let me go out back alone. Inside the storage shed, which was piled high with a bunch of junk my aunt knew she didn't need, I glanced toward the back, looking for the panel. I tapped on a few panels per LaQuanta's instructions, then noticed the one that was loose. I pulled it back and noticed a duffle bag. I snatched the bag out, opened it, and gasped at the sight of all that cash. My shock turned to anger as I tried to come up with some rational reason why my cousin had all of this at his mama's house.

I initially took just the five hundred thousand, but just as I was closing the panel, I remembered this was my money, so I reached back and grabbed the rest.

It had taken an act of Congress to get away from Aunt Ora after that because she insisted that I let her wrap me up some chicken and dumplings to take with me.

I know I needed to get to LaQuanta's, but I wasn't a complete fool. There was no telling what kind of crazies I was about to go see, so I swung by my house, ran and stashed the three-hundred thousand dollars in the attic, and headed back out.

It didn't take long before I was pulling up in front of LaQuanta's dilapidated apartment on the Southwest side. I looked around, recalling how when I was growing up, this used to be a nice area. But now, low income housing and people who didn't value their property had turned it into a cesspool.

I texted LaQuanta to let her know I was outside and five minutes later, she came strutting out like she was walking out the Ritz Carlton. With her loud burgundy hair, tiny waist and butt that looked like it had seen one butt injection too many, I wondered what my cousin saw in this girl. Granted, he wasn't a prime catch, but I definitely thought he could do better than her.

"You got the money?" LaQuanta said, sliding into the front seat.

"Yeah." I had so many questions for Darnel and as soon as he was safe and sound, he wasn't leaving my sight until we went to the bank and withdrew all of my money, or what was left of it anyway.

"Cool, get on I-10 she said, toward downtown."

"Who are these guys he's mixed up with?" I asked as I pulled off.

"Fat Freddy is a drug kingpin," she said nonchalantly.

"Drugs? Since when did Darnell get into drugs?" I screamed.

"Oh, he don't do them. But you know, now that he has a little change, he figured he could flip a little somethin', somethin', double his money, and walk away rich. Darnell is straight-laced. He don't even smoke weed, but I told him this was a good idea."

I gasped as my head snapped in her direction. "What? So this was your idea?"

"Look, I ain't know he was gonna get jacked for ten keys."

I didn't even know how much ten keys was but it sounded like a lot.

"Jacked? So someone stole the drugs?"

She nodded. "Yep. He'd just picked it up. Hadn't made one sale when he got jacked. He tried to tell Fat Freddy, but that pig wasn't hearing it. He wanted his money, and then Darnell started running off at the mouth and told them about his stash."

"I just can't believe this," I said. Darnell had been to jail before, but for minor stuff – stealing a pack of cigarettes, DUI – nothing major. So why he thought he could run drugs was beyond me.

"I'm just glad you came through, though," LaQuanta said. "I thought you might take the money and run."

"Yeah, since it is my money."

"Whatever." She waved my comment off. "I told him you were gonna be pissed and just take the money, but Darnell said, no matter what, you were family and would come through for him."

"Where am I going?" I asked, just ready to get this day over with.

"Head toward Fifth Ward. They got him in a trap house over there."

"So, I'm about to go into Fifth Ward with a duffle bag full of money? Why don't we just call the cops?"

She looked at me, appalled. "Because we ain't no snitches, number one. Number two, Fat Freddy would put a bullet in Darnell before you finished pressing the 1 in 9-1-1."

I wanted to cry. How did I go from my meager little life to a husband that was on the verge of suing me, and a cousin wrapped up in drugs, kidnapping, and who had a loudmouth girlfriend who I wanted to kick out my car?

LaQuanta's phone started ringing just as I exited the freeway. I shook my head at her ring tone of Usher's "I Don't Mind."

"Yeah," she said, answering. "Chill, I got it. Me and her on our way. Let me talk to Darnell. . . Man-Man, if you don't put my man on the phone."

She pulled the phone away from her ear, then pressed the speaker button. There was some rumbling, then, "Say something!"

"Quanta?" Darnell sounded horrible. Like he'd been to hell and back.

"Hey, baby," she purred.

"Where you at?" he said, his voice hoarse.

"On our way to get you, bae, so you hang on, okay?"

I couldn't help it. I interjected. "Darnell, are you okay?"

"Yeah, cuz." He sounded so weak. The part of me that wanted to clean cuss him out, now only wanted to hug and protect him. "I'm sorry, J-Bug," he said, using the name he used to call me when we were little. "I got caught up. I'm so sorry."

"Darnell, just hang on," I said. "We're on our way, okay?"

Suddenly, it sounded like someone snatched the phone. "Y'all better hurry up," a deep male voice said. "I ain't got all day."

"Chill, Fat Freddy," LaQuanta said. "You 'bout to be rich."

"I'm already rich, trick."

"Well, you 'bout to be richer," she said. "Even though you know you wrong marking up product 500 percent."

"Whatever. Just get here before your boy get capped. I already wanna put some panties on his weak ass. Cryin' like a lil' punk."

That's because my cousin isn't a thug, I wanted to scream. Instead, I just floored the accelerator. "Just let them know not to hurt my cousin. We'll be there in fifteen minutes."

At that moment, the money didn't matter. I just wanted to save my cousin. . . so I could then kill him for the hell that he'd put me through.

Epilogue – Six Months Later

Angelique

This should've been a celebration. But instead, it looked like we were about to film an episode of the reality show, "The Lottery Ruined My Life."

At least Raquelle was managing to look on the bright side of our lotto headaches. She was the only one sitting there, seemingly at peace as we sat around the table of The Cheesecake Factory. Raquelle had just filled us in on how our former boss had basically stolen her money in exchange for her freedom. She'd told me a few weeks ago, but this was the first time that we'd all gotten together since we'd won the lottery eight months ago.

"I still say, you should've fought Mr. Perry. He didn't even need the money. He was just being dirty," Terrance said. "I mean, that was bonafide extortion. That's illegal."

Raquelle shrugged. "Yeah, but so is embezzlement and I turn Mr. Perry in, saying he tried to extort me, he gets a slap on the wrist, and he fights like crazy to make sure I go to jail. I couldn't take that chance," she replied, shaking her head. "It's like my mom said, I had just enough money to do what I needed to do. That's the blessing I need to focus on. My son went to a baseball game today with a neighbor and I got to see him off." She was smiling, but tears peaked out as she continued. "That is priceless and if I had to give up every nickel to see that, then so be it. Shaun's care is paid up, I don't have a record, so I was able to find another job."

"I can't believe you have gone all this time without telling us," Terrance said. "You know I would've given you some money."

"Awww, I appreciate that." Raquelle replied. "But you're gonna need your money, especially with that newborn."

"Don't remind me," he said, groaning as he picked up his drink. Terrance Mays, Jr. had come three weeks early and was 99.9 percent Terrance's child. Mia had done a DNA test the day she gave birth. She'd sent a copy to Terrance and one to Sheray, just in case Sheray was thinking of taking her husband back. Of course, that solidified everything for Sheray. She filed for divorce. And that sweet "I just wanna love you" person who didn't want any parts of his money, took him for half.

"I can't believe I'm trapped with this woman for the next 18 years," Terrance said.

"I can't believe your nasty tail slept with that girl without protection," I said.

"I did use protection," Terrance replied. "But as Mia reminded me, we had sex three times that night, yet I only had two condoms. I was too drunk and too caught up." He took another swig of his drink. "And now, I'm paying the ultimate price."

"Well, if you lay down with dogs, you'll come up with fleas," I said.

"Thanks, Angelique," he said, his voice laced with sarcasm.

"At least y'all still got your money," Janine said, finally speaking up. We'd had to drag her out to dinner today. She'd been holed up in her house for months. She'd taken a job at a call center for one of those online colleges, so she'd sunk into a deep depression. I was stunned when she filled me in on the made-for-TV drama involving her cousin, Darnell. She'd had to shell out half a million to some drug kingpin to save his life. Darnell ended up safe and Janine ended up with less than four million dollars. Apparently, Darnell had blown through nearly two and a half million bucks. How that was even possible in that short time, I didn't even know.

And what Darnell didn't get, Tony did.

"I can't believe Tony took your money and filed fraud charges against you," Terrance said.

Janine had told us how Tony had dragged her to court and since she didn't want to lie under oath, she'd confessed how she was the actual winner and had her cousin claim it. Janine had been forced to give Tony half of the original winnings – roughly four million – almost everything she had left. The good thing in all that was that Tony was still taking care of their son, so it wasn't like they were suffering. "Is he still with that girl?"

"Nah," Janine said. "He took the money and made a demo. I heard he got it in front of some producer and while they're not feeling his rapping, they do have him doing some writing for other artists."

"Wow," Raquelle said. "Maybe his music career will take off and you'll be set anyway."

Janine looked like those words gave her little comfort. I felt compelled to speak up and let her know that money hadn't equated to happiness for me.

"Well, I may still have my money, but it's not the same when you don't have that special someone to share it with," I said.

"How is Marcus?" Raquelle asked.

"I don't know. I called him a few times, but he doesn't call me back. I finally got the message, he was done with me." Just thinking about it brought another pang to my heart. "I haven't seen him in months."

"Umm, looks like that's about to change," Terrance said.

"What are you talking about?" I asked.

Terrance motioned across the restaurant to the hostess stand. Marcus was leaning against it, going through his phone. He looked better than ever in some crisp Sean John jeans, Tims and a polo.

"Girl, go talk to him. Tell him, you're sorry, that you've learned your lesson. Whatever you need to do. That's a good man and you need to get him back," Raquelle said.

"Raquelle is right. It's obvious you've been miserable. Well, fate has intervened," Janine told me. "Go fight for your love."

"Love sucks," Terrance chimed in.

"Don't listen to Bitter Billy," Raquelle said. "Go get your man."

I thought about what they were saying. I missed Marcus something terribly. It wasn't Antonio that I thought about constantly, it was my life with Marcus that I longed for. I stood, took a deep breath, checked my appearance in the wall mirror, then made my way over.

"Marcus?" I said, approaching him.

He seemed surprised and genuinely happy to see me. "Hey, Angelique." He hugged me. "How are you?"

"I'm okay. You?" I didn't know why I was so nervous. I'd lived with this man for four years. Why was my stomach fluttering like this was a first date?

"I'm doing good. Everything okay with you?"

I nodded. And an uncomfortable silence hung between us.

Finally, he said, "You look great."

That made me smile. "I managed to keep the weight off. Hit 110 pounds down last week."

"That's awesome. I know that's what you really wanted. So I'm happy for you." The expression on his face told me he meant that.

"Marcus, I mi. . ." Before I could finish my sentence, a woman walked up and draped her arm through his. "Hey, baby, sorry about that. I'm ready to go."

He smiled at her. A loving, caring smile. The type of smile that used to be reserved for me. "No problem," Marcus said.

I was speechless as I stared at the woman . . . all three hundred pounds of her.

"Babe, this is Angelique," he said.

Her eyes lit up. "Oh. I've heard so many things about you," she said with a wide grin. She extended her pudgy hand and my eyes were drawn to the big rock that looked like it was squeezing the life out of her ring finger.

"Angelique, this is Tonya," Marcus said.

Tonya kept her smile as she said, "His fiancée."

I had no words. Her bold declaration made Marcus uncomfortable, as I'm sure he knew that he had just driven a dagger through my heart.

Tonya seemed unfazed when I didn't take her hand. She just dropped it and kept talking. "Marcus told me about your history. I have to say thank you for letting him go." She squeezed him tight. "Because honey, he is my knight in shining armor. I just love this man." She leaned in and kissed him. "It didn't take me but a few weeks of dating to know that he was the one. I can't wait to give him lots of babies. Can you believe he told me he wants five?"

Yes, I could believe it because when he'd told me that, all I could think was, *do you know what five babies would do to my body?*

I knew this whole Chatty Patty performance was a lioness staking her claim. And as tacky as it was, I couldn't say that I blamed her.

She continued, "But I'm sure marriage and babies are the last thing on your mind with all that money you won." Marcus grimaced and she either didn't notice or didn't care. "Girl, I know winning the lottery made you happy. Me, I'm a simple girl. I just want a man that loves me for me and I want to spend my days loving him back."

I was so glad when Marcus finally spoke up. "Well, Honey, we need to let Angelique get back to her seat." He forced a smile. "It was good to see you, tell everyone hello." Then, he hurried his fiancée away.

I couldn't believe I was still frozen in place until I heard my friends behind me. "Are you okay?" Raquelle asked.

"No," I whispered.

"Awww, Sweetie," Janine said, rubbing my back.

I'm not gonna cry. I'm not gonna cry, I told myself as I watched them walk out of the restaurant into the Galleria Mall.

I forced a smile as I turned to face my friends. "It is what it is," I said, even though my heart was crumbling as we spoke. "I made my bed . . ."

"Hey, cheer up. You're so fine, that you'll have another man in no time. Shoot, if I didn't know how crazy you were, I might holla at you myself," Terrance joked.

That made me laugh and I appreciated him trying to lighten the mood. "No thanks. I don't do baby mama drama and trust, you're about to have a lot of that." I dabbed my eyes and took a long, deep breath. "No, maybe I need to do like Marcus once told me, and love myself before I go searching for someone else to love me."

"Well, shoot, we're in a mall. I know how you ladies are – a little retail therapy should make you feel better," Terrance said. "So, let's go shop."

I glanced over the railing, and saw Marcus and Tonya walking hand in hand.

"Nah, there are some things I want that money can't buy."

Each of my friends nodded. We'd all learned that. The hard way.

If you enjoyed

Pay Day,

We're sure you'll like

Touched By An Angel

By

Victoria Christopher Murray

And

Princess F.L. Gooden

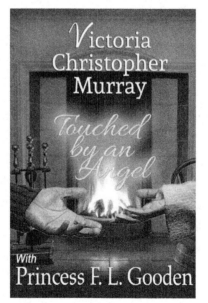

Enjoy this excerpt. . .

Chapter One

With the bare tips of my fingers, I lifted the red thong from my husband's suitcase, slowly, deliberately as if it were a pit viper. My lips parted into a wide O as I stared at the lace underwear, panties that I'd never seen before.

It wasn't like I was searching for trouble; in the twenty-three years of my marriage to Sheldon, there had never been anything close to drama in our relationship, especially not this kind. The two of us were solid, the kind of couple that Ashford and Simpson sang about back in the day when as a teenager, I dreamed about the man who would take my hand after my father walked me down the aisle. That man had been Sheldon Hudson – and he'd kept every single one of the vows we'd shared on our wedding day.

At least that's what I'd always thought.

I took a deep breath, just to make sure that I was still alive.

Why am I still holding onto these? I wondered.

But even as I had that thought, I could not release the death grip the tips of my fingers had on the panties. In my mind, I imagined the woman who owned this strip of material and I could almost see myself – twenty years younger. I could hear myself – with a high-pitched tone that belonged to someone who had not yet fully stepped into womanhood. And worse – I could see Sheldon – grinning as the tramp sauntered toward him wearing nothing more than these five inches of silk and lace. And maybe a pair of matching stilettos.

I snatched myself from that nightmare and shook my head. How in the world had I ended up here? After all, it wasn't like I was sneaking around, rummaging through my husband's bag as if I was a wife with no trust. No, I was doing what I'd always done when Sheldon returned home from a business trip.

Like all the other times, the car service had dropped him off in front of the house less than an hour ago and he had dragged himself and his bag across the trace of snow that sprinkled the path to the front door of our Capitol Hill townhouse. His eyes were blood-shot with exhaustion from the red-eye flight he'd taken from Los Angeles.

But even though he was tired, he'd kissed me with every bit of energy he had left and I followed him as he dragged his suitcase up the spiral staircase to the second level of our home.

Inside our master suite, Sheldon had dropped his luggage at the foot of our bed, tossed his briefcase and cell phone onto the bed, then staggered into the bathroom.

While he relaxed under the double heads in our steam shower, I had eagerly unzipped his bag in search of my gift. Years ago, he'd given up hiding my surprise – now, he laid it on top for me to uncover quickly. From perfume to pearls, he always brought home something that put a smile on my face and gratitude in my heart. And today, just days away from Christmas, I couldn't imagine what I would find.

And... well, I had never expected to find this!

The sound of the shower shutting off, snapped me from my shock and my head twisted toward the bathroom. Through the closed door, I heard Sheldon singing his favorite song.

I believe in you and me...
I believe that we will be...
In love eternally...

When the movie, *The Preacher's Wife* had hit the big screen, Sheldon had declared that this song was our song.

As he sang, I could tell he was rejuvenated and refreshed; inside the richness of his tenor, I heard his anticipation.

I did the only thing I could – I stood still and waited until the door opened and Sheldon stepped out. His damp skin glistened and his smile was just as bright. The towel tucked at his waist was loose as if he didn't plan for it to stay there long.

"Hey, baby." His greeting was filled with the lust that always came from being away from home for five days.

Still grasping it with just my fingertips, I held up the thong. "What is this?" I asked. I didn't even recognize my own voice – my tone was as deep as my husband's.

His smile rolled upside down and he squinted, trying to see what I held. "What's what?"

My heart pounded with a pain that made me want to fall to my knees. But, I pressed through it and held the underwear higher – straight in front of his face for his eyes to see what mine had seen.

His frown deepened. "What's that?" he asked again as if he didn't know.

I had hoped for more from the man who had promised that he would forsake all others. I had expected my upstanding husband to confess right away that he'd fallen and quickly beg for my forgiveness. Maybe then, there would have been a slither of a chance that I would forgive him and we could somehow find a way to move on.

But now, there was no chance of reconciliation. Not if he was going to play me like this. Not if he was going to lie and deny.

The words of my three-time-divorced best friend came to me now.

"Men cheat, and then they lie. That's what 'man' stands for - men-admit-nothing."

Theresa had lost her faith in men a long time ago, even though I constantly worked to get her to see that all men weren't the same. And, I always held up Sheldon as Exhibit One. But now it seemed like Theresa was the one who needed to be schooling me.

"Savannah, sweetheart." His voice was full of the same confusion that was etched deep in the lines on his face. "What *is* that? Why are you showing me those..."

"Don't you dare do that, Sheldon," my voice quivered as I interrupted him. "Don't you dare stand there and tell me that you have no idea what these are." I shook the cloth between my fingertips.

"I don't."

Raising my hand high, I tossed the satin and lace toward him; the thong hung for a moment in the air before landing at his toes. "Whose are those?" I screamed. "Who do those panties belong to?"

He held up his hands, shook his head. "I don't know what you're talking about."

"I'm talking about you bringing your whore's underwear into my home."

"What?" Now, his voice was as loud as mine.

"I'm talking about you cheating on me. How could you do this?" I cried.

"I don't know what..."

I didn't let him finish. "Don't deny it, Sheldon!" I screamed. "I found those in your bag; I'm not stupid, I know what those panties mean."

Now, he said nothing. And, it was the way he stood silent that made me snap. That made me rush to him with my fingers clutched into fists, ready to attack. But he grabbed my wrists before I could begin my assault.

"I can't believe you did this to me!" I said. "After all these years. After all the love that I've given to you. After *everything* that I've given to you." Fury gave me the strength to wrestle free from his grasp and I pounded my fists against his chest.

His eyes widened at my punches and he tried to push me away.

Stammering, he began, "I...I...I..."

The beginning of his confession came out in a gurgle. "I...," he said again before his legs shook, his knees bowed, he fell to the floor, the towel now completely free.

I stood there for a moment, confused. Was this really the way Sheldon was going to handle this? He was going to pretend that he fainted?

But then, it was the way he laid there, his eyes rolled back, his fingers clutching the skin on his chest.

Now, it was my eyes that widened and I dropped to the floor.

"Sheldon!" I sounded different now. Yes, I shouted, but my voice was filled with panic.

His mouth opened and his eyelids closed.

"Sheldon!" I pressed my fingertips against his neck, felt his pulse, then jumped from his side. Rushing to the nightstand, I grabbed the telephone.

"Help me, please," I exclaimed to the 9-1-1 operator. "My husband. He collapsed. I think he's had a heart attack!"

Want more? Order your copy at

www.BrownGirlsBooks.com

And while you're there, make sure you sign our mailing list so we can keep you up to date on future releases.

CPSIA information can be obtained at www.ICGtesting.com
Printed in the USA
LVOW04s1520220715

447215LV00017B/809/P